The Veil and the Crown

Book II

The French Sultana

The French Sultana

Zia Wesley

Copyright 2014, Zia Wesley
Print Edition published by Zia Wesley 2014
Editing by Mark Burstein and Ariane Wolfe
Cover design by **Clark Walker**
based on the painting *A Harem Beauty*
by Henri Guillaume Schlesinger
(French Artist b 1814 d. 1893)
Print formatting by **A Thirsty Mind Book Design**

ISBN: 978-1500642556

For more information about the author please visit:
www.ziawesleynovelist.com

Dedication

This book is dedicated to
Caliph Abdul-Majid Kahn II,
last Sultan of the Ottoman Empire,
and all of the descendants of Nakshidil Sultana.
I hope I've told her story well.

The Veil and the Crown:

Book 1

The Stolen Girl

Summary

Aimée Dubucq de Rivery and her cousin Rose Tascher de La Pagerie grew up on the island of Martinique during the last quarter of the eighteenth century.

Based on a prediction by the seeress Euphemia David, both girls fantasized about one day marrying handsome aristocrats and living fashionably in Paris.

Aimée's dreams were shattered after she failed to be accepted by Parisian society. Consequently, she decided to become a nun. Before taking her vows, she embarked on a farewell journey to Martinique to visit her family one last time. Several weeks into the voyage, her ship was attacked by Algerian corsairs who were fascinated by her exotic Safire blue-eyes and golden hair. They brought her to Algiers where they sold her to the captain of all pirates, Baba Mohammed Ben Osman, the infamous Dey of Algiers. Hoping to ingratiate himself politically, Ben Osman gave her as a gift to the aging Sultan of Turkey.

As The Stolen Girl ends, Aimée has embraced her fate and entered the harem where she was given a new name: Nakshidil. Within five days, she finds favor with the sultan and becomes the new favorite. She moves into her own lavish apartments within the seraglio and begins a new phase of her education guided by the Circassian Kadine, mother of the heir and ruler of the harem. However, Aimée's meteoric rise to power as the new favorite creates an angry furor among the sultan's five hundred concubines and infuriates the one who has the most to lose...Nuket Seza, mother of the sultan's first born son. Her lust for power is boundless and she has already eliminated every newborn child for the past seven years.

Rose believed her dreams had come true when she sailed to France to marry the aristocratic lieutenant Vicomte Alexandre de Beauharnais, but he quickly dispelled all of her fantasies of happiness. Within two years after her marriage, Rose is pregnant with her second child and suing her wayward husband for financial support. She and her daughter, Hortense are living outside of Paris with her Aunt Désirée Renaudin. She recently wrote to Aimée to tell her about her desperate situation.

List of Historical Characters

Aimée Dubucq de Rivery, who becomes Nakshidil, "The French Sultana" and Valide Sultana, Queen Mother of the Ottoman Empire

Marie-Josèph Rose Tascher de La Pagerie, who becomes Rose de Beauharnais, then Empress Josephine Bonaparte

Euphemia David, "The Irish Pythoness," *obeah* woman (seer) of Martinique

Rose Claire des Vergers de Sannois, Rose's mother

Joseph Gaspard Tascher de La Pagerie, Rose's father

Désiré Renaudin, Rose's aunt

Vicomte Alexandre de Beauharnais, Rose's first husband

Hortense de Beauharnais de Bonaparte, Rose's daughter

Eugène de Beauharnais, Rose's son

The Emperor Napoleon Bonaparte

Archduchess Marie-Louise of Austria, Napoleon's second wife

Eléonore Denuelle, Napoleon's mistress who gave birth to his first illegitimate son

Countess Marie Lontchinska, Napoleon's mistress who gave birth to his second illegitimate son, Alexandre-Florian-Joseph, Comte Colonna Walewski.

Jacques-Marie Le Pére, Chief engineer with Napoleon's Egyptian campaign

Czar Alexander I, Czar or Russia

Sultan Abdul Hamid, Sultan of the Ottoman Empire when Aimée enters the seraglio

Mihrisah, The Circassian Kadine, Valide Sultana, mother of the heir Selim

The Kizlar Agasi, chief black eunuch in the Sultan's harem

Baba Mohamed Ben Osman, Dey of Algiers, Captain of all Barbary pirates

Selim, nephew of Sultan Abdul Hamid and son of The Circassian Kadine, who becomes Sultan Selim III

General Aubert du Bayet, unofficial French ambassador to Turkey during Sultan Selim's reign in 1796

Mahmud, son of Sultan Abdul Hamid and Nakshidil, who becomes Sultan Mahmud I

Baron Francois de Tott, a Hungarian serving as a general in the French army who advised the Ottoman Turks in military matters during Sultan Mahmud's reign.

Mustapha, son of Sultan Abdul Hamid and Nuket Seza, who becomes Sultan Mustapha IV

Nuket Seza, mother of the first-born son, Mustapha

Pierre Ruffin, French chargé d'affaires in Istanbul

Baron Horace François Bastien Sébastiani, first French ambassador to Turkey

Fanny Sébastiani, wife of Horace

Mufti Vely Zade, a wealthy Turkish ally to the Sultans

Marie Le Normand, French spiritualist and biographer of the Empress Josephine

Koca Yusuf Pasha, Grand Vizier of the Ottoman Empire

Besma, bath attendant and favorite of Sultan Mahmud, who gives birth to six of his children

Ibn-Abd-al Wahhab: founder of Wahabbism

Muhammad Abd Ibn Saud: head of the powerful Al Saud tribal family.

Map of the island of Martinique

Map of Aimée's Journey

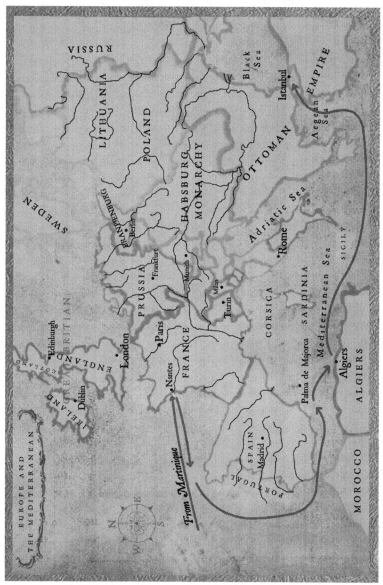

The French Sultana

Zia Wesley

Chapter 1

Following a short period of drunken and confused deliberation about how to best eliminate the new favorite, Nuket Seza the emotionally unstable Baskadine (mother of the heir), settled upon the plan she always chose. Her attempts to focus on the exact number of women and babies she had poisoned in the last eight years always left her irritable. *Was it ten boys and three girls or three girls and ten boys?* Holding figures in her head made it ache and it did not matter anyway because she was going to poison the little blonde whore's food. Her personal Kutuchu Usta (herbalist) reminded her that serbets were the easiest food to alter since they were not cooked. One simply added the poison to the drink before it was served. Nuket remembered using a poison serbet in her attempt to rid herself of the Sultan's annoying nephew, Selim, and would have succeeded had his mother's meddling Kutuchu Usta not administered an antidote so quickly. She smiled to herself and thought, *the new li'l whore has no Kutuchu Usta to interfere, does she?*

"Poison her in the hamam," she told her herbalist.

As the woman left to do her bidding, Nuket Seza congratulated herself, confident that her problem would be solved and the new girl would soon be dead. But shortly before the noon meal, her spies reported that Nakshidil, the new favorite, had not returned to the baths.

"She bathes privately," one woman said.

"With the Circassian Kadine," added another who cowered away from her reach lest she strike.

"Old Kadine," she growled. "Meddling whore."

She tried to digest the new information carefully. If the girl couldn't be poisoned in the baths, she would have to die during one of the meals.

Nuket lolled in her private pool, trying to decide at which meal she should eliminate the girl, when another of her spies burst in with even more disturbing news. Nakshidil had been summoned to visit the Sultan for a second time.

"Second visit?" she exclaimed. The sultan had not summoned any girl for a second visit in many years. Her mind began to spin wildly out of control. She hauled her substantial girth out of the water and stomped angrily back and forth along the pool's edge. "Arak!" she screamed.

Within minutes a servant arrived bearing a bottle and a small crystal glass. Without interrupting her frantic pacing, Nuket knocked the glass from the servant's hand and grabbed the bottle, tipping it to her lips to drink deeply. "Must kill the li'l whore fast," she muttered aloud.

Swallowing another gulp, she made her decision. Since serbets were not served at breakfast, the first opportunity would be the following day's noon meal. She summoned her Kutuchu Usta, and instructed her to poison Nakshidil's first serbet on the following day. Feeling pleased with her own cleverness, she flopped down onto a divan and finished off the remaining Arak then passed out, to her servants' great relief.

Had she known Nakshidil would leave the harem for her own apartments, she would certainly have poisoned her morning yogurt instead. But the newcomer's promotion had occurred so quickly that by the time Nuket rose from her inebriated slumber the following morning, the new favorite was already gone.

The Baskadine fumed. It would now be much harder to slip poison into *anything* she ate because her food would come from her private kitchen, served by her own servants. It was going to cost her a small fortune to bribe the people she needed to do the job now.

Her blood pressure rose quickly along with her anger, as her face turned crimson and her head began to throb. The foiling of her plans was bringing on one of her horrendous headaches, and she shrieked in response, sweeping all of her glass unguent bottles from their shelves with one huge arm, sending them smashing onto the floor.

Upon hearing the breaking glass, eight-year-old Mustapha immediately ran to his special hiding place—the one he used to protect himself from his mother's worst rages. His mother searched frantically. When she could not find her son, she flogged one of her servants instead, and as her emotional state spiraled out of control, forced her to drink the poison intended for Nakshidil. Within minutes, the servant's contorted body writhed on the floor in agonizing pain. Watching the woman's painful death seemed to be the only thing that finally enabled the Baskadine to calm down. When the death throes ceased, she summoned her eunuchs to remove the body.

The suspicious eunuchs asked politely how the woman had died.

Nuket Seza casually shrugged and replied "Must have eat something bad."

No one in her service who knew the truth would ever dare to tell lest a similar fate be visited upon them.

~ ~ ~

Had Sultan Abdul Hamid been more like his predecessors, he would have had his gardeners strangle Nuket Seza and Mustapha long ago. That was the preferred method used by Sultans for hundreds of years to rid themselves of treasonous officials, unpleasant wives, and relatives who might one day pose a threat to the throne. But Abdul Hamid thought the practice barbaric, and had never employed it himself. He disliked murder almost as much as the *Kafes* [cage] in which he had resided for fifteen years before assuming the sultancy.

The Cage had originally been designed as a way to protect heirs from the traditional practices of fratricide and infanticide. It was a tall, narrow, three-story brick building, void of windows on the ground floor. Once incarcerated within its walls, all contact with the outside world was forbidden. Deaf mutes served as guards, cooks and servants. If an heir came of age while residing there, a few odalisques were admitted—and remained imprisoned. No education, culture or entertainment was allowed and the heir was kept ignorant of political and current events. No human contact or nurturing was provided. As a result, a boy might be incarcerated at the age of seven and released at the age of forty to assume the sultanship—most often, as a deranged lunatic. Ottoman history was filled with the horrifying deeds of such men.

When Abdul Hamid was incarcerated, he was fortunate to have been thirty-five-years old, well educated, and quite cultured. Still, fifteen years of deprivation left its mark, mostly in that it prevented him from imprisoning Mustapha. However, had he known of Nuket Seza's intentions to kill Nakshidil, he would surely have made an exception for her, as well as her son.

Ignorant of the brewing storm, the Sultan happily installed his new favorite in the third largest apartment in the palace, conveniently connected to his own by a secret passageway directly behind his massive bed. He ordered the Kizlar Agasi to oversee the furnishing of her new quarters and notified the Chief Treasurer, to begin paying her a generous monthly stipend. The Kizlar Agasi would advise the new favorite on how to best invest her fortune. He would also manage her properties and those of any children she might bear. Through the coming years, Nakshidil would amass a large fortune in her own right.

After the Sultan finished giving the orders regarding Nakshidil, he notified his chamberlain of his intention to ride out to the Hagia Sophia mosque that evening. It was an old established custom for the Sultan to pray in one of the city's public mosques on Fridays. Abdul Hamid had not done so for six months.

On such an occasion, a large retinue of ministers, important women of the harem, and the Grand Vizier accompanied him. The Sultan's horse was covered in jewel-encrusted cloths for all to see, unlike other public appearances when the tall-feathered turbans of the eunuch guards blocked him from view. Quite often, as many as ten thousand citizens and foreign visitors crowded into the First Court to watch the procession.

~ ~ ~

Given their first opportunity to leave the harem in six months, the women rushed to prepare themselves. They primped and preened, bathed and scrubbed, hennaed and coiffed, then donned their finest clothes and jewels, despite the fact that they would be completely covered.

Nakshidil and the Circassian Kadine did not attend the march to prayer, preferring instead to organize the new apartments. However, Nuket Seza took advantage of the occasion to be "seen" in the Sultan's presence. Everyone knew that the woman who walked in the most honored place, directly behind the Sultan's horse, was the Baskadine, mother of the first heir. Consequently, she spent the entire day in preparation, devoted two full hours to the choice of her ensemble, and finally settled on her gaudiest purple ferace. The unfortunate result was startling.

"She looks like a giant shiny eggplant," one of her servants whispered to another as she departed.

As the procession passed through the Gate of Felicity towards the mosque, Nuket Seza followed closely behind the Sultan's horse to insure her vaulted position. Out of breath, and trotting to keep up, she strained her neck in a futile attempt to see over the horse's rump. She huffed and puffed, grateful when the Sultan's horse stopped a few yards from the steps of the mosque. Bracing her hands on her chubby knees, she bent forward to catch her breath, as the stallion lifted his tail to drop a steaming pile of dung at her feet.

Immediately understanding what had occurred, the Sultan maintained his composure, smiled broadly and nodded at the gathered crowd.

Her bejeweled kid slippers now splattered with manure, Nuket summoned her eunuchs with one shrill command. They quickly surrounded her, shielding her from the snickering crowds, and made their way back to the seraglio. She fumed silently as she walked, her mind spewing vengeful thoughts and curses. *He gonna pay for this. His baby gonna die.*

~ ~ ~

The news of Nuket Seza's public humiliation quickly reached the Circassian Kadine who immediately mobilized her loyal harem spies. She could imagine how infuriated Nuket would be by Nakshidil's new position. Certainly, there would be other women resentful of a girl who had captured the Sultan's heart in just five days, when they had spent years being overlooked. Nuket Seza might easily enlist these disgruntled women to support her in some act of jealous retribution. To safeguard against this, the Kadine instructed Nakshidil's new eunuch guards, and chose a trustworthy Kutuchu Usta to serve her personally.

The Kadine then summoned a small army of palace artisans—upholsterers, furniture makers, glass blowers, carpet sellers, and drapers—to Nakshidil's new apartment. The men were led through the harem blindfolded, and received by the women who were completely covered. Eunuchs, outnumbering the craftsmen three to one, stood guard as the new occupant chose suitable furnishings.

At one point, Nakshidil entered into a discussion with a furniture maker who did not seem to understand her request.

"A chair," she repeated for the third time.

Turning to the Circassian Kadine for help, she asked, "How do I say 'chair' in Turkish?"

"There is no word for chair because we do not have such a thing. Of course we had chairs in Circassia." She stopped to think for a moment. "Perhaps we might draw a picture of one to illustrate."

Together they drew a chair resembling the Rococo style that had been fashionable in Paris during Aimée's visit. It was square, with a high backrest ornately carved and gilded in gold leaf, with a plump, down-cushioned seat. She wished it to be upholstered in deep magenta velvet.

The furniture maker looked at the sketch and asked,

"And the purpose of this piece is?"

"To sit upon," Nakshidil replied.

Mystified, the man simply agreed. It was not his place to question the Sultan's women, and he had fashioned stranger objects for other odalisques. He would be well paid whether or not the things he made were useful or comfortable.

"I would like two chairs," Nakshidil said to the artisan.

"So that you may sit with me when you come to visit," she added to the Kadine.

~ ~ ~

That evening the Kadine instructed Nakshidil in the protocol and attire required for her visit to the Hall of the Divan on the following day. She must wear a plain black ferace and yasmak so as not to be visible through the pierced wall. The Kizlar Agasi would escort Nakshidil and secrete her within the "Eye of the Sultan," before leaving her to join the council. In order that her presence remain unknown, she would enter through the private door used only by the Sultan and his chamberlain, prior to the council's arrival.

Due to her early admittance, she would not observe the elaborate processional entrance made by the Divan members and the Sultan. Therefore, the Kadine described the procedure that had been followed for three hundred years. Just after daybreak, the council members of the Sublime Porte, as the government was called, gathered in the First Court with their retinues of clerks and guards. According to Ottoman law, each man was attired in the robe, turban and boots specified by his rank. Uniforms comprised a rainbow of colors, with feathers, furs, turbans, conical hats and a wide variety of swords, knives and weaponry. Group by group, the members slowly marched five hundred yards across the courtyard to the Gate of Salutation. When the entire group had assembled at the gate, they proceeded into the Second Court, where as many as ten thousand Janissaries, gardeners and gatekeepers stood to watch them pass. Passing into the Second Court, the officials formed two long lines, making a pathway for the Grand Vizier and the Sultan into the Hall of the Divan. As a sign of reverence, the men stood with their arms crossed over their chests and downcast eyes that never looked directly upon their sovereign.

Once inside the Hall of the Divan, visitors were always overwhelmed by the opulent splendor—the intended purpose. The floor and walls were gilded in pure gold, and set with hundreds of precious jewels that glittered and sparkled in the sunlight that poured through the glass-domed roof.

Chapter 2

From her secret place behind the pierced wall, Nakshidil could see why the room was called "The Golden Chamber." The brilliance of reflected sunlight made it almost too bright to see without shading one's eyes. She watched the men solemnly enter and take their places on divans, while the Sultan reclined upon his throne, looking healthier and more alert than he had during their previous encounters.

As the proceedings began, Nakshidil listened intently so that she could later report accurately what transpired to the Circassian Kadine. She hoped the information she passed on would prove useful to whatever purpose the heir's mother might have. She also fully intended to learn more about the machinations of this mysterious government.

In the first order of business, the Sultan had previously revoked some minor but long-held rights of the Janissaries, who considered any type of change a threat to Islamic tradition. They believed Allah's laws to be perfect, irrevocable and never subject to change; that the government of the Ottoman Empire was the political expression of those laws. Consequently, the government could not change. Traditions were meant to be followed, not altered or broken.

Nakshidil had never been witness to any such event. The Kizlar Agasi recited the council's approval of the Janissaries' new demands, and then moved on to the next order of business.

The Sultan sat quietly throughout the proceedings, occasionally glancing in Nakshidil's direction to see if he could discern her presence. But his new odalisque sat well back from the lattice wall and did not move.

When the council adjourned and the room emptied, the Kizlar Agasi escorted Nakshidil back to her apartment.

"My lady Nakshidil," he said. You performed a very valuable service today for which many people will be grateful."

"I am happy to be of service, sir, and I found it very interesting."

"Nakshidil," he said bowing deeply, "you are now 'my lady,' and I am no longer 'sir.'"

Surprised by his obeisance, and still unfamiliar with her new power, she laughed and then quickly regained her composure. "By what name shall I call you?" she asked.

"I am called Beyazid, after a Sultan who lived almost four hundred years ago. He was defeated in battle and punished by being carried before his people in a cage. Soon after, he conquered those who had enslaved him."

"Conquered those who enslaved him," she mused aloud. "A fitting name for the man who rules the sultan's harem, I would say," she smiled.

"Yes, my lady. I hope that you enjoy your new home and that you will allow me to fulfill any and all needs you may have. I see now why my old friend Baba Mohammed held you in such high esteem. With your permission, I will send him news of your good fortune."

She was delighted by the mention of his name. *Dear, dear Baba,* she thought fondly.

"Oh, yes, thank you. I wish that I could write him a letter myself. Might that be possible?"

The eunuch smiled wistfully. He hoped that power would not corrupt the graciousness of the lovely young woman, whose life was about to change so dramatically. "It seems that almost anything is possible now, my lady. I will personally assure your letter's delivery. And now, I bid you good evening."

Alone for the first time in her new surroundings, Nakshidil surveyed each room carefully. There were five rooms in her suite, and two additional small rooms for her personal servant, Zahar. Her favorite was the sitting room that opened onto a small enclosed garden with fruit trees standing along a bubbling stream. A tiny gilded kiosk sat next to a little pond covered with pink water lilies and bordered by rows of red tulips. Rose bushes grew along a walking path that she knew would be well used and in spring and summer the doors could remain open, allowing sweet, fragrant air to fill her rooms.

Nakshidil's small dining room had a glass dome in the ceiling through which both the sun and moon would shine. She stood for a moment gazing up, remembering the dome in Baba's house that had opened to the night sky, and made a mental note to see if such an opening might be possible here. The lower portions of the walls were tiled in intricate patterns of flowers and birds, the upper portions covered by delicately carved wooden panels.

While she was familiarizing herself with her new home, one of the Circassian Kadine's servants arrived to ask if the Kadine might call on her.

~ ~ ~

A few minutes later, the two women reclined in Nakshidil's salon.

Getting right to the point, the Kadine began, "I have had word from the harem that concerns me. Nuket Seza is furious that you have gained the status of 'favorite,' and plans to do you harm."

Nakshidil was shocked. "Do me harm?"

Zahar entered with a tray of coffee and sweets.

"Who prepared this coffee?" the Kadine asked.

"I did, my lady," Zahar replied.

"And the sweets?"

"From the harem kitchen," she replied.

"Throw them away and do not taste them yourself. They may be harmful."

Zahar nodded, and took the sweets away to dispose of them.

"Nuket Seza intends to poison you," the Kadine said.

Nakshidil stared at her in disbelief. She had never had an enemy or anyone who wished her harm. Now a woman whom she had never met wanted to kill her. "To *poison* me out of jealousy?" she whispered.

"Oh no, my dear. It is much more complicated than simple jealousy. Despite the Sultan's contempt of her, Nuket Seza has successfully maintained the position of the most favored woman in the harem for eight years by eliminating any woman or boy child who threatened her position."

"But how?" Nakshidil asked.

"Through successive acts of treachery...including murder."

"Murder? But surely there are laws to prevent or punish such behavior."

"My dear child, the seraglio is an empire unto itself and, unfortunately, these practices have existed and been accepted for hundreds of years."

"But it is so..." she searched for a word that would not sound insulting.

"Barbaric? Yes. The Turks are famous for their barbarism, despite their sophistication in other matters. If you remember, it was Nuket Seza who poisoned Selim. She is stupid, but wealthy enough to pay others who are smarter than she. I have made arrangements with my personal food taster to serve you until you can engage someone yourself, and you will dine with me tonight. Remember at all times, wherever you are, eat nothing that has not first been tasted and drink only those things that have been prepared by Zahar. Be especially wary of serbets."

Nakshidil found it difficult to comprehend that someone wished her dead. "What shall I do?' she asked.

"For now, we must be wary and take precautions." The Kadine rose and paced the room thoughtfully. It would be wise to find a way to render their nemesis helpless. "I will consider this problem and discuss it with Beyazid."

She knelt before Nakshidil's divan and took her hand. "You are too young and kind-hearted to understand the twisted mind that plots against you. I am no longer burdened by either so you must rely on me in this." The Kadine rose and returned to recline on her divan.

"Let me tell you something of Nuket Seza. Her mother was poor and terribly abusive to her seven children, most of whom were, unfortunately, girls. Nuket never knew what happened to her father; whether he died or simply left the family. She was the youngest. When she was ten years old, her mother had no way to pay the local healer for the traditional circumcision customary with their North African tribe, so she performed it herself...truly mutilating the child. It is a miracle she survived. Before the terrible wound had time to heal, the mother sold her to a slave trader from a passing caravan, who immediately prostituted the girl to his passengers." She paused to take a sip of coffee and allow her words to be fully comprehended.

Nakshidil simply stared at the Kadine in horror.

"I understand it normally takes up to three months for this type of wound to heal and as I said, the mother did it herself, so the result was more horrific than usual. I have seen it and cannot imagine how painful it must have been. Apparently, the initial coupling was so painful to her she fiercely fought off the customer, attempting to scratch out his eyes. So, the caravaner fed the girl opium to deaden the pain and make her more pliable. She was sold or traded to other caravans like that several times, and traveled throughout North Africa until she was fifteen, when she was sold into the harem. It is hard to imagine how beautiful and exotic she was then, like you in some ways. Of course, she was not blonde but very different from most of the other women because of her great stature and African blood. The Sultan had only been on the throne for a short time and was still in the process of sampling a different woman every night. There were only forty women in the seraglio then, and many were chosen without ever spending time in the school for odalisques. Nuket was one of these and as fate would proscribe, she was the first to become pregnant and to bear a male child."

Aimée thought of her own childhood and, for the first time in her life, felt fortunate. Her parents had not left her alone intentionally; both had died young, and despite her aunt's selfishness and indifference to her, she had not been physically abused. She would never have imagined feeling pity for someone as cruel as Nuket Seza. But she did.

The Kadine continued. "When her son was born, the wound of her mutilation was reopened and despite the best efforts of our doctors, it could not be properly repaired. She suffered a great deal for many months afterwards and, unfortunately, took all of that out on the boy, whom she blamed for her pain. I believe that her rage and the continual beatings she inflicted on the boy turned him into a sadistic bully. He is a terrible child who will no doubt grow up to be an equally terrible man." The kadine paused and shook her head sadly. "These days, Nuket prefers strong drink to opium because the drink allows her to indulge her gluttony while the opium takes away her appetite. So, she drinks Arak all day and smokes opium to sleep. Unfortunately, drink does not dull her anger like opium, and she is prone to uncontrollable fits of rage. I believe the only time she has any peace is when she sleeps."

Moved by the story, Nakshidil's eyes had filled with tears. "Is there no way to assuage her pain and anger? It is whispered her child is a monster, and how could he be otherwise? How can this possibly end well for either of them?"

"It will not end well, my dearest. We can only hope that it will somehow end soon."

Nakshidil sighed deeply. "I am sorry for her and for her son. I will pray for their salvation."

"You would do better to pray for their demise. I foresee no salvation here. Meanwhile, try not to fret. The Kizlar Agasi has chosen your guards from the ranks of men who cannot be bought at any price, and I have posted extra guards outside your garden doors. You will be safe here."

Nakshidil's brow furrowed. "I feel like a prisoner...for the first time."

"Not so, my girl, you are a cherished member of the royal family, who must be protected."

The Kadine stood to leave. "Have your guards escort you to my apartment tonight to dine." She bent to kiss Nakshidil's cheek, and left.

When Nakshidil was alone again, she reclined on a divan, reflecting on the complex subculture that had been hidden from her until now. If she intended to survive, as well as rise in the harem ranks, she had much to learn, and the first thing she must do was surround herself with loyal companions. She must remember to ask the Kadine if it might be possible to bring Perestu, her young friend from the harem school, into her service.

~ ~ ~

The next two weeks were filled with activities to complete her apartments, the hiring of a personal staff, and almost nightly visits to the Sultan. The latter occupied most of her time, as she was forbidden to wear the same attire more than once. Consequently, she spent several hours each day with her dressmakers, and several more in the bath being prepared: massaged, exfoliated, oiled, shampooed, hennaed, perfumed, made up and coiffed.

The Circassian Kadine advised her against speaking to the Sultan about Nuket Seza until they had proof of her intentions. One did not burden the sovereign with rumors, as there were more rumors in the harem than there were women.

"She will show her hand in some way," the Kadine assured her. "Or a servant will become frightened enough to bear witness against her. Be patient, and take good care."

Chapter 3

Early one morning at the end of November, when Nakshidil had been in the harem for almost six weeks, she lay atop the linens on her bed, pale and listless. Fearing that Nuket Seza had finally succeeded in her evil intent, she barely found the strength to summon her Kutuchu Usta to her bedside. How had this happened when she had been so careful? All of her food was prepared in her private kitchen by trusted cooks, and then tasted by her personal food taster. When had she been remiss?

The loyal herbalist arrived, and Nakshidil whispered, "I am not well, Mahine. I could not eat my yogurt this morning, and my stomach feels as if I am at sea."

Fearing the worst, the wise woman asked, "What have you eaten or drunk today?"

"Just rose-petal tea that Zahar prepared for me."

"When did you last eat?"

Nakshidil thought for a moment. "Yesterday, at the noon meal. I had no appetite for dinner, and awoke so ill this morning." She closed her eyes, certain that poison coursed through her body and that she was dying.

Mahine felt Nakshidil's forehead, which was cool to her touch. She gently pressed her fingers into Nakshidil's belly above the navel. "Does that hurt?"

"No."

She moved her hands, and carefully palpated Nakshidil's abdomen. "Any pain here?"

Nakshidil shook her head, no.

"Here?"

"No."

"Let me see your tongue," she said, examining it closely. "Do you have pain, anywhere?"

"No, but I think I'm going to be sick."

The Kutuchu Usta quickly pulled a large silver tray from a bedside table, and held it for Nakshidil to vomit onto. When the retching stopped, she took the tray to another room to examine its contents, while Zahar tended to Nakshidil.

Several minutes later, the Kutuchu Usta returned to find Nakshidil propped up against her pillows and faintly smiling.

"It is odd, Mahine, but I feel fine now."

The herbalist raised her eyebrows knowingly, her suspicion confirmed. "When did you last bleed?" she asked.

Nakshidil frowned in thought. *Well, the last moon was...*she silently calculated in her mind. "I always come into cycle..." her words trailed off as the reason for her sickness dawned on her. "Last week. I should have bled last week," she said, her face breaking into a smile.

Mahine gently squeezed Nakshidil's hands. "You are fine, my lady. Stay in bed this morning, and I will bring you a special tea to calm your stomach. You must not immerse yourself in the hot baths for the next five months. Take only warm baths. I will tend you daily with teas and herbs to make you and the baby strong and healthy."

Tears of joy filled Nakshidil's eyes and dropped onto her cheeks. She heard Euphemia David's prophetic words as clearly as if the old Obeah woman were in the room with her. She smiled at Mahine and said, "I am going to have a son."

"Well, my lady," Mahine said, "you are certainly going to have a baby."

"No, Mahine, I am going to have a son."

The older woman nodded. Sometimes women knew the sex of their children before they were born. "I will notify the Saray Usta to certify the pregnancy, but there will be no doubt. The Sultan has summoned you almost every night. Rest now, and I will bring you some tea," she said, patting her hand.

When she was alone, Nakshidil pressed her hands gently against her belly.

When will I be able to feel him?

She felt instantly transformed from one being into two.

A child is growing in my body…a son.

Despite her broad smile, tears rolled down her cheeks. She felt as if her joy might burst out and fill the room with magical colors or music. Hugging her belly, she rolled onto her side laughing.

I am going to have a son. Oh, how I wish I could tell Rose. I must find a way to tell Rose…and Baba. Won't he be surprised?

When the Saray Usta was informed of Nakshidil's condition, she dutifully checked her register that documented visits to the Sultan. The record prevented a pregnant girl from illegally claiming a royal conception. If someone other than the Sultan impregnated a harem girl, the penalty was death. However, the Saray Usta rarely heard of these mishaps, as most women terminated unwanted pregnancies with certain herbs. Unfortunately, jealous rivals were also able to terminate the pregnancies of others without their knowledge. Once the news of Nakshidil's pregnancy spread, her life would be in even more jeopardy.

Due to the high rate of miscarriages, women were forbidden to divulge a pregnancy to a Sultan until the first two months had safely passed.

Although unaware of Nakshidil's condition, the Sultan enjoyed the swelling of her little breasts. He assumed that she was eating more, as he had requested, and his ardor increased along with her weight. Nakshidil laughed at his obvious passion, remembering Perestu saying "the Sultan like round woman." The thought of her little friend made her smile, and she told the Kizlar Agasi that she wished to have the girl near her.

"I shall arrange to have the child join you in the harem as soon as possible," he assured her.

Delighted by the prospect of being with her friend, Nakshidil arranged to install Perestu in a large room that adjoined her own apartments.

One week later, Perestu followed the Kizlar Agasi through the harem's maze of hallways to Nakshidil's apartment. Forgetting the appropriate protocol for addressing the Sultan's favorite, the young girl ran into

Nakshidil's arms and hugged her tightly.

"Namay, Namay, I miss you so much," she cried.

Nakshidil was touched to hear her old name spoken and did not correct the girl. "I missed you too, little sparrow. Let me see how much you've grown," she said, holding the girl at arm's length. She shook her head from side to side in mock disappointment. "We shall have to fatten you up. Remember, the 'Sultan like round woman.'"

They spent the entire afternoon talking about everything that had happened to them since they had last met.

"And what of love?" Perestu asked.

Taken aback by the forthright question, Nakshidil replied, "Love?"

"Yes. You love the Sultan?"

"I do not think so, but perhaps I do. He is kind and gentle and happy to grant my every wish. Many evenings we talk for more time than we make love," she replied.

"Maybe this is love," Perestu said thoughtfully. "Do you ever love someone different from this, Namay?"

She thought for a moment. "There was a young man on the ship whom I thought I might have loved." Her voice trailed off as the old pain crept into her chest. She had not thought of him in a long time, and could still picture his handsome face and hear the strange inflection of his brogue-tinged French. "Mr. Braugham," she whispered.

Perestu saw the pain her query had caused. "I am sorry, sister," she said, reaching out to hold Nakshidil's hands. "I never know love. It hurt, yes?"

Tears rolled down Nakshidil's cheeks. "I don't really know." She wiped her tears, and attempted to smile. "I doubt I know anything at all of love."

~ ~ ~

By the end of her second month of pregnancy, Nakshidil felt quite well. The morning sickness and afternoon fatigue had begun to subside leaving her with a new found energy. Anxious to share her news with the child's father, she requested a special audience following the noon meal.

Nakshidil entered the Sultan's chambers dressed in rose colored silk, with the Sultan's sapphires strewn through her hair. She knelt, touching her forehead to the floor.

Surprised by her formal approach, the Sultan rose from his divan and walked to her, extending his hands to help her rise.

"Nakshidil, why do you prostrate yourself so? What is wrong?"

She smiled and replied, "Nothing is wrong my lord—quite the contrary. You are going to be a father again."

His face contorted as if he could not comprehend her words. "Nakshidil," he whispered.

She grasped his arm, thinking his legs might give out, and helped him to a divan.

"I did not think that you could make me any happier. I never dreamed." He shook his head in disbelief. "But you are the one who must rest," he said, rising and helping her to recline in turn. "You must rest and take special care. I shall call my physicians at once."

Nakshidil laughed. "If you wish, my lord, but I am quite well. My Kutuchu Usta has been taking care of me for two months, and says that I am perfectly healthy. I do feel very well—excellent in fact, although I am constantly hungry."

He sat on a footstool by her side and kissed her hands "You shall have everything you need, my love, anything you desire. You have made me happier than you can ever know."

She gave his arm a little tug to bring him onto the divan beside her, and in a conspiratorial tone whispered, "My Lord, I believe I carry your son."

Overwhelmed with emotion, the Sultan stroked her cheek and smiled. "My son…may Allah make it so."

He noticed how radiant she looked, and wondered why he had not guessed at her condition himself. *Well, I have only seen one pregnant woman, and Nuket Seza never looked like this.*

Word of Nakshidil's pregnancy spread through the harem like fire through a barn. However, fearing the punishment they might receive as bearers of bad news, none of Nuket Seza's spies was willing to tell her. Consequently, it was purely by chance that she overheard women discussing the pregnancy in the communal baths. She had gone there desperate for an evening's diversion, and never imagined she would hear such horrible news.

Feeling angry and embarrassed to be the last to know, she made an uncharacteristic effort to control her temper, lest the other women discover her ignorance. Gritting her teeth together, she left the baths as quickly as she could, her mind silently screaming, *the li'l slut...pregnant.*

What could be more demeaning than failing to learn the harem's most important secret? That was what she paid her spies for. *Why didn't they tell me? Worthless lying curs. I paid them well. Now* they *will pay.*

The Baskadine waddled down the halls to her apartments, and once safely inside, let out a screeching stream of obscenities that sent Mustapha and her servants fleeing. She smashed anything breakable within reach, as her blood pressure soared and her head began to throb. Sweating profusely, and unable to catch her breath, she ordered a servant to bring her a bottle of Arak.

She was desperate to eliminate the girl. She needed to think. Since thinking was a task for which she had little facility, she drank Arak, hoping to stimulate her less than clever mind. Unfortunately, it never produced the desired effect.

Unable to organize her scattered thoughts, Nuket chanted the same phrase repeatedly, like a mantra, "Must kill li'l whore's baby. Must kill li'l whore's baby."

When two bottles of Arak had been emptied and she still had not devised a plan to eliminate her rival, she rolled onto her stomach, vomited onto the floor and passed out.

Nuket Seza's servants quietly cleaned up her mess, sickened by the stench but careful not to awaken the sleeping dragon.

A few days later, Nuket used Mustapha in an attempt to gain entrance to Nakshidil's apartment, believing the guards would not suspect a child. But Nakshidil's guards were familiar with the boy's malevolent nature, and barred him from entering.

His mission thwarted, Mustapha smashed the glass of poisoned serbet against Nakshidil's closed door, and cursed the guards vilely as he slunk away to secrete himself in his safe hiding place. His mother might kill *him* for failing. He needed time to invent a lie to throw the blame onto someone else.

Chapter 4

During the next three months of Nakshidil's pregnancy, Nuket Seza made several more unsuccessful attempts to poison her. The continual disappointments fueled her habit of drinking Arak, and she quickly began to deteriorate. Even the women whose "friendship" she had bought found it painful to witness her self-destruction. In her disturbed mind, the new favorite became the sole reason for all of her pain and failure. Obsessed with her desire to destroy Nakshidil, and too drunk most of the time to control her tongue, she voiced her hatred, as well as her plans, to anyone willing to listen.

It would have been impossible for her behavior to go unnoticed by the Baskatibe, the harem secretary in charge of conduct and discipline. Nuket Seza's position as Baskadine could never be changed—she would always be the Mother of the First-born, but the leniency her position afforded was not infinite. Constrained by the laws of protocol, the secretary watched and waited, certain that a punishable crime would eventually be committed, and hoping it would not be the death of the Sultan's favorite, or his unborn child.

At least Nuket Seza's indiscriminate outbursts kept

the Circassian Kadine abreast of her plans, and allowed Nakshidil to stay ahead in the treacherous game. However, the constant threats were taking a toll on Nakshidil. It frightened her to realize she had begun to understand Nuket Seza's motives, and that she herself was, of necessity, becoming cunning.

~ ~ ~

Now in the sixth month of her pregnancy, she awoke early one morning and sat among the soft silk pillows on her bed, sipping rose-petal tea. For the hundredth time, she thought about Euphemia David's prediction. She had previously not believed that every aspect might come true, but at present no doubt remained. She pondered the part about her son's reign preceded by "the blood of his predecessor." *Does this refer to the death of Selim or Mustapha?*

She now understood that the sultan's nephew, Selim as the eldest male was the rightful heir. Nakshidil also knew that Nuket Seza would never cease her efforts to eliminate him in order to raise her own son, Mustapha to that position. The struggle for power would never cease as long as Nuket Seza and her son lived.

What if Nuket Seza succeeded in killing Selim?

The thought sent a chill up her arms. She took a sip of her tea and had an odd thought. Perhaps it was she, and not Nuket Seza, who would determine her unborn son's fate. If that were true, and her son's fate rested *in her own hands*, what must she do? She closed her eyes and the answer was clear: the "blood of his predecessor" would be spilt by her own hand. As Mustapha was next in line before her own son, it must be his blood that is spilled. *Am I truly thinking this?* Another chill made her body shake, and she hugged her shawl closer around her shoulders.

She remembered being in the convent, romantically pondering the possibility that life might hold "more" for her than she suspected, but that girl could never have imagined any of this!

~ ~ ~

The larger Nakshidil's belly grew, the more protective she became of her unborn son, and the more resolved to take action. She made preparations to keep the baby with her at all times, arranging for a milk mother and a nurse to live in two small rooms adjoining her apartments. Then she instructed masons to seal both doors that led to the outside, making the only access to the nursery through her private rooms. Her suite would be an impenetrable fortress, and she its guardian.

Many times she wished that she could call upon Euphemia David, and wondered if the seer were still alive. She considered sharing the prediction with the Circassian Kadine, but feared she might disapprove. Unfortunately, Nakshidil had not yet discovered that many women of the harem practiced "the black arts"—foretelling the future—or that the Circassian Kadine herself spent an inordinate amount of time with one of them, a young Greek girl gifted in palmistry.

The girl's name was Sholay, and she had been in the

seraglio for three years. From her earliest days in the Cariye Dairisi, she had openly shown a preference for girls. The Kutuchu Usta made this known to the Circassian Kadine, who casually replied, "She will most likely outgrow it. So often girls prefer other girls until they experience a man."

However, during her final tests, Sholay had become wildly infatuated with the Circassian Kadine, and during a moment alone, made her feelings known. The Kadine passed the girl, hoping to pursue the mutual attraction within the "safer" confines of the harem.

A short time later, following their first tryst, Sholay read the Kadine's palm quite accurately, further endearing her to the older woman.

During the months that followed, Sholay's feelings became so strong she begged the Kadine to keep her for herself, rather than present her to the Sultan. The request was the first of its kind ever received by the Kadine, whose favor was usually courted for the opposite purpose, an introduction to the Sultan. Although Sholay was not the first lover the Kadine had taken in the harem, she was the only one who lacked the desire to advance her own position.

Perhaps it was Sholay's guileless attraction, or simply the girl's voracious sexuality that eroded the Kadine's usual defenses. Whatever the cause, the result was clear. For the first time in her life, the Circassian Kadine felt the bittersweet pangs of love, and allowed herself to be vulnerable with another human being. They shared their most intimate thoughts, fears, and feelings and, for the first time since the birth of her son, the Kadine felt truly happy. Since offering herself as a teenager, the Kadine had never allowed herself to imagine she might ever find love. Instead, she had sought and found power. Now, at the advanced age of forty-one, she was unexpectedly disarmed by the love of a young woman.

Within the harem, the intricacies of any illicit love affair were always complex and dangerous. The Kadine enjoyed more freedom because of her position and more importantly, was not one of the Sultan's women. Unfortunately, this was not true for Sholay. Since the penalty for an unfaithful odalisque was death, both women were careful to keep their relationship hidden. For a little more than a year, they had loved each other with the utmost discretion, or so they believed.

Had Nakshidil spoken of Euphemia David's prediction to the Circassian Kadine, she would surely have called upon Sholay to read the girl's palm. But the women who practiced the "black arts," like illicit lovers, also practiced discretion. They were sometimes called upon to do more than just *predict* an outcome, and punishment for working their craft could be as mild as imprisonment or as severe as death. Should anyone who wished to do her harm learn of her clandestine activities, Sholay's life would be jeopardized on two counts.

~ ~ ~

As Nakshidil's pregnancy flowered into the seventh month, the opportunity that Nuket Seza sought finally arrived with an older serving woman whose malice was fueled by her lack of power and favor.

It was noon, and Nuket Seza was enjoying her third meal of the day, gnawing on the leg of a pheasant. She barely acknowledged the woman who stood before her, bowing deeply.

"I have good news, my lady."

"How much?" Nuket Seza asked without looking up.

The woman wrung her hands nervously. "Oh, very valuable news, my lady. Very valuable indeed."

Nuket Seza continued ripping flesh from the bird's leg. "Ten gold pieces. No more."

"That is very generous, my lady, very generous, but my information is worth so much more, I assure you."

Nuket Seza had been inundated with useless bits of gossip for six months, paying for secrets that never led her anywhere. Nakshidil was still alive and pregnant, while *she* was just angrier and poorer. She flung the gnawed bone onto the floor and wiped her mouth on the back of her hand. "Ten pieces or nothing. Speak or get out."

"Ten pieces, yes. However, I should like to propose that should you see the value of my news, and if by chance it leads to the solution you have been seeking, that one hundred pieces of gold might be more appropriate."

Nuket Seza began to shift her body as if she might get up, and the spy backed away and began speaking rapidly.

"There is a young girl, Greek girl, Sholay. She is the

lover of the Circassian Kadine."

The Baskadine's mind was not facile enough to immediately grasp the implications of this news, but she was, nevertheless, intrigued. "She tell you this?" she asked.

"No, one of her young slaves. The slave has accompanied her on many visits, and bragged of it to me."

Now the Baskadine was beginning to see the possibilities this information might afford. Nakshidil also visited the Kadine, and if the two were there at the same time, she could make the Greek do the job for her. "Sholeg, you say?"

"Sholay, my lady."

Nuket Seza signaled her servant to bring a small silk purse from which she extracted ten gold coins. She held them in her open, greasy palm for the informant to take. "If her and baby dies, you be paid well."

The woman took the coins and smiled broadly. "Thank you, my lady. Thank you. You will see I am right." She bowed several times, and then left.

"Arak!" Nuket Seza yelled. "Must think now," she muttered to herself.

~ ~ ~

Later that afternoon, after drinking only half a bottle of Arak, Nuket Seza miraculously devised a plan. She summoned Sholay, who entered her apartments a short while later.

For the meeting, Nuket Seza adorned herself in what she believed to be her most imposing and regal garb: a sparkling red silk ensemble topped with white ostrich plumes coming out of her headdress. She powdered her face white, and rouged her lips, cheeks and eyelids bright red, making her look like a gigantic, frightening porcelain doll. As Sholay entered, the Baskadine smiled broadly, displaying a mouthful of uneven, yellow teeth, rotted from the copious amounts of sugar she consumed, and indicated that Sholay make herself comfortable on a divan across from her own. With her typical lack of subtlety, she wagged a fat finger back and forth and said, "You have li'l secret, girl." Her face contorted into a mock frown. "Bad li'l girl."

Sholay wondered which of her secrets had been discovered, but maintained a blank expression and said nothing.

Nuket Seza stuffed her mouth with dates as she spoke. "Bad li'l girl gonna die if secret get out, huh?"

Sholay was appalled by the woman's lack of manners and slovenly appearance. Hoping that a calm demeanor might outwit her accuser, she quietly replied, "I do not understand."

Nuket Seza threw her head back and laughed loudly, then abruptly turned angry. She pointed at Sholay and yelled, "Filthy lovemaking wit' Circassian Kadine. Unnerstan' that?"

The blood drained from Sholay's face, her worst fear confirmed. *What does she want?* She froze.

Nuket Seza smiled. "You gonna do li'l favor for me so no one gonna know, an' you keep alive. Unnerstan'?"

Sholay nodded tentatively, despite the fact that she did not understand at all. Better to agree than to anger the horrible woman.

"That good." She filled her mouth with sugared almonds. "You see li'l favorite, Nakshidil, with Circassian Kadine?"

Sholay's brow furrowed. She was not sure what the woman was asking. Did she think that Nakshidil was also the Kadine's lover? "What do you mean?"

"You there in Kadine's apartment when Nakshidil there?"

"No, we have not met," she answered honestly.

"Liar! She there all the time. Li'l whore good frien' wit' bitch Kadine." Chewed almonds spewed from her mouth with each word. "You poison favorite or I tell secret. Unnerstan'?"

"You want me to poison Nakshidil?" she asked incredulously.

"That's right," she nodded emphatically. "You poison or I tell secret. You die." She laughed at her own cleverness. "She die or you die. Unnerstan'?"

Sholay's instincts told her to agree. Nuket Seza was obviously not a woman with whom she could either argue or disagree. She nodded her head. "Yes, I understand."

"That's good. You wait now."

Nuket Seza summoned her Kutuchu Usta, who had been waiting in the next room. Holding aloft a purse of gold, she motioned the woman to take it. "Bring poison for food," she said as the herbalist took the purse and left.

A moment later, she returned carrying a small glass vial of dark liquid. Nuket Seza motioned her to hand the vial to Sholay, who grasped it gingerly between the tips of her fingers as if it might bite.

"Get out," was all the Baskadine said to end the meeting.

Sholay's hand shook as she secreted the vile in her girdle and left. She walked a few feet, then leaned against the wall of the passageway to steady herself and wait for her legs to stop shaking.

Is she mad? How can she expect me to kill an innocent woman and child? What would lead her to believe that I might do such a thing? But, if I don't, am I willing to die in their place?

She walked down the long, narrow corridor, keeping an eye over her shoulder as she went, making sure no one was following, and went directly to the Circassian Kadine's apartment.

Initially pleased by her lover's unexpected visit, the Kadine's smile quickly faded when she noticed the girl's strained expression and heard the tone of her voice.

"We must speak privately," Sholay whispered.

As soon as the Kadine's servants were gone, Sholay handed her the vial.

The Kadine took it, and looked into the girl's eyes. "Where did you get this?"

"Nuket Seza. She has threatened to expose us if I do not…" She could not even finish the sentence.

"For Selim or Nakshidil?'

"Nakshidil."

"She is more clever than I thought," the Kadine said, as she began to pace back and forth. Thinking aloud, she said, "I cannot go to the Baskatibe with this proof without exposing you. Yet, if you do nothing, Nuket will report you." *Either way, my lover is doomed.* "I must think. Meanwhile, let her believe that you are waiting for the right moment to do her bidding." She hugged Sholay and kissed her cheeks. "Do not fear, my love. I will find a way to protect you. No harm will to come to you. I will not allow it."

When Sholay had gone, the Kadine went out to her private garden. She walked along the gravel paths, touching one exotic blossom after another, sometimes bending to inhale their intoxicating fragrances. She felt as if someone had taken a needle and pricked a delicate bubble within her heart, allowing all of the joy to escape at once.

Is this how it feels to lose a loved one?

It was a pain she had never known. At the very end of the garden, where she was sure to not be seen, she sat on a marble bench and wept until evening turned the garden cold and dark. Then she returned to her apartment and smoked her opium pipe until she fell into a drugged, dreamless sleep.

The next morning, she instructed her servants to not admit visitors. She needed to find a way to save both Nakshidil and her beloved Sholay, to protect herself, and to end Nuket Seza's threats permanently. She was sorry that it was not her nature to harm others, or she would have ended the problem sooner, after Selim's poisoning. Her orthodox upbringing was clear on the consequences of committing murder, and she did not wish to spend eternity with the damned. There had to be another way—and she was determined to find it.

Chapter 5

13 May 1783

My dearest cousin Rose,

I pray that this letter reaches you from the hands of Mssr. Pierre Ruffin, chargé d'affaires in Istanbul, and that you and your family are in good health and high spirits.

So much has transpired since last I wrote, I feared it might take hundreds of pages to tell in its entirety. It is a miracle I am able to send this to you at all.

As you must already know, when I sailed from Nantes almost two years ago, my ship was set upon by Algerian corsairs (as had been foretold). I was frightened beyond words whilst in their charge, although they neither molested nor harmed me. We sailed to Algiers, where I was delivered into the hands of an extraordinary gentleman named Baba Mohammed Ben Osman, the Dey (Mayor) of Algiers. Miraculously, he spoke French, and what might have been my untimely end became, instead, my new beginning.

I remained five months as an honored guest in that gentleman's palatial home, and through his kind guidance and tutelage, became familiar and quite comfortable with Turkish customs and language. After furnishing me with a wardrobe and dowry befitting a princess, we sailed to Istanbul, Turkey, where I entered the seraglio of Sultan Abdul Hamid.

Do not despair, dear Rose, for all aspects of Euphemia David's prophecy have thus far come true, and I write to you not from a prison, but from my own lavish apartments within the most beautiful palace you could imagine. I am, at present, the Sultan's favorite, and carrying his child—a son, I have no doubt. Although the Sultan bears no resemblance to the husband I imagined in my youth, he is a kindly gentleman, who treats me as a "queen." I want for nothing. Can you believe, dearest cousin, the foreseen events that have come to pass?

Which leads me to inquire of you, dear Rose. How are your children and has your unhappy situation with your husband been resolved? As so much of my prophecy has come to pass, I wonder about yours. Please, reply so that I know this has reached you, and be so kind as to convey my news to our aunts, Lavinia and Sophie. I am well and happy. I know it will be hard for you to imagine how I might say such a thing (because we had such foolish notions of what it might be like here), but I assure you that those we believed to be barbarians are, in fact, quite civilized in most things, and that I am not held against my will.

I close with the fervent hope you hold these pages in your hands soon, and that we begin a correspondence from our different worlds. I have been assured that since Mssr. Ruffin's post has been established, mail will ship on a timely basis between here and France.

I remain, as ever your devoted cousin,
Aimée Dubucq de Rivery
Post script: my Turkish name is Nakshidil, which means "embroidered on the heart."

It had taken the Circassian Kadine three days to design a plan that would serve her needs: to save Sholay's life, to protect herself as well as Nakshidil and her unborn child, and to render Nuket Seza harmless without having to kill her. As soon as all the pieces had come into place, she summoned the Kizlar Agasi.

Her appearance surprised him. No jewels adorned her simple, dark blue robes, and her face looked drawn and tired.

"Mihrisah, I was beginning to fear that something terrible had happened. Why have you secreted yourself alone here for these past days?"

"I apologize for causing you undue concern, but there has been much to contend with and I needed to think. Now I will tell you a story that, I pray, may have a somewhat happy ending. Rest, my friend," she said, indicating a large divan close to her own.

She ordered coffee served, and then dismissed her servants.

"Nuket Seza has finally given us the opportunity we have prayed for, but it comes at a terrible price to me." She paused to sip her coffee and regain her composure, still devastated by the thought of losing Sholay. "Had she not underestimated my resolve, it might have gone in her favor, but I believe I have found a way to turn the tides."

She began by revealing Nuket Seza's attempted blackmail. Of course, he had been aware of the Kadine's affair with Sholay from the beginning—it was, after all, his duty to know who was sleeping with whom. But he had guarded her secret, rather than use it against her.

"Who is the informant?" he asked.

"We do not know…not yet."

They spent the rest of the afternoon refining the intricacies of their plan, and by dusk the two old friends had become co-conspirators.

~ ~ ~

The following evening, according to plan, the Kadine summoned the secretary, the Baskatibe, to her quarters, where Sholay knelt at her feet with her head bowed.

"Tell her what you just told me," the Kadine coldly instructed Sholay.

"Forgive me, my lady. I feared for my life," Sholay whispered.

"Tell her, you deceitful wretch," she commanded.

"I was trying to poison Nakshidil."

The Baskatibe gasped. "Why would you do such a thing? Did someone put you up to this?"

"I fear to say, my lady."

"You had better say if you wish to be spared. The person who bade you do this, will pay with her life. You may live yours out in prison if you give me her name," the Baskatibe said.

"Prison? I shall die in prison."

"You shall die either way," the Baskatibe said. "One way sooner than the other."

"Nuket Seza bade me do it."

"And paid her well," the Kadine added, holding out

a small wooden box filled with jewels. "It was just by luck I discovered her sneaking into my hamam disguised as one of my bath servants."

"Nuket...of course, the treacherous witch. We will all be well rid of her. Remain here while I fetch the guards to deal with you," she told Sholay, leaving the room.

As soon as she had left, the Kadine knelt before Sholay and took her face in her hands. "Drink quickly, my love," she instructed, and kissed the girl deeply on the lips.

With tears in her eyes, Sholay extracted a small glass vial from her girdle, uncorked it and tipped it to her lips, draining the vial completely. Within seconds, she collapsed onto the floor and the Kadine rose to her feet and screamed, "Help! Call the Kizlar Agasi!"

The Kadine stood helplessly over the young girl's body until the Kizlar Agasi and a retinue of his guards arrived. Feeling for the girl's pulse at her neck and finding none, he declared, "She is dead. Take her away."

"Report this to the Baskatibe," the Kadine said coldly. "I want nothing more of this treachery tonight. Leave me now."

"Very good, my lady," the Kizlar Agasi responded with a bow, and then followed his guards from her rooms.

"Bring my pipe," she told her servant, "then leave me until morning."

The Kadine willed herself not to cry, and tried to remain focused on a good outcome, as she reclined and smoked deeply. Almost immediately she entered her comforting dream world where all thoughts and feelings were enveloped in a lovely, soft fog, and the only sound she heard was her own breath. Soon, even her vaguest thoughts disappeared into the mist, and she rested.

~ ~ ~

Her plan depended upon a dangerous herb, well known in the lore of Turkish folk medicine. When ingested, it produced symptoms that mimicked death. If administered properly, the deathlike state lasted only a short time; if not, actual death could result. The Kadine's Kutuchu Usta had used the potion only once, with good results.

Immediately following the certification of Sholay's "death," a handpicked detachment of the Kizlar Agasi's most trusted guards removed her body from the seraglio. Under the cover of darkness, they delivered her to the Mufti Velly Zade's palace on a hill overlooking the city, twenty kilometers from the seraglio. The Mufti was one of the Sultan's oldest and most loyal supporters. Sholay would be safe there, and if the rest of the scenario went as planned, one day she might be able to return to the harem.

The Circassian Kadine would explain that the girl had taken her own life by drinking the poison intended for Nakshidil. The empty vial of poison and the box of jewels would serve as evidence, and no one would have reason to question the word of the Kadine, certainly not over that of Nuket Seza. It was a perfect plan.

While the Kadine rested in her induced stupor, an official tribunal marched ceremoniously into Nuket Seza's apartments. One eunuch forced her to her knees while another read the charges: She was accused of attempting to poison the Sultan's favorite and causing the death of the woman she bribed to carry out the deed. The Baskadine would be banished to the Palace of Tears on the following day and her son Mustapha, would be incarcerated in the Cage. Out of courtesy for her position, they allowed her to spend the remainder of the night overseeing the packing of her personal belongings. Dumbstruck by the news and too confused to understand the unexpected turn of events, Nuket Seza swayed on her knees, and slowly shook her head from side to side.

As soon as the officials left her apartment, she struggled to her feet and called for a bottle of Arak. Her addled brain found it difficult to fully comprehend the facts, but two things were clear. Her son was going to the Cage, and she was going to the Palace of Tears, where she would be powerless to ensure his assent to the throne. No arm was long enough to reach out from the Palace of Tears. Her only chance to achieve the power she craved would be gone forever. She would be abandoned and forgotten. *Abandoned and forgotten,* she thought. *Just like before.* What could she do?

Panic seized her and an idea came into her head. She grasped at it like a drowning person reaching for a floating log. She must find someone to kill Selim—kill him while she still could. Kill the heir and put Mustapha on the throne. But how? She had been trying to kill him for years. Her mind would not cooperate. She drank glass after glass of Arak, becoming drunker and drunker in her attempt to think more clearly.

"Need help," she mumbled. "Fetch Safay and Soraya here now," she slurred to one of her servants.

The frightened servant dared not disobey. She went into the harem and tried in vain to entice the women she had summoned to meet with her mistress. But the news of Nuket's banishment had already reached the would-be conspirators who wanted to distance themselves as quickly as possible, lest they be made to accompany her in exile. Both women firmly declined. Too frightened to report this to her mistress, the servant did not return to the Baskadine's quarters.

When no one appeared, Nuket decided to handle the matter herself, and stumbled drunkenly into the elegant hamam.

Standing unsteadily in the doorway, her corpulent body swaying from side to side, she screamed, "Who gonna help me kill the scum Selim?"

All activity abruptly stopped. The stunned women made no reply.

"I pay good," she slurred, as she tore at the strands of jewels around her neck, precious stones spilling onto the floor at her feet.

No one moved or spoke.

"He must die!" she screamed, as several eunuchs physically removed her from the baths. "Must DIE!"

~ ~ ~

By early the following morning in the hour before dawn, Nuket Seza began to sober a little, and in doing so, realized her defeat. She rose laboriously from her divan and systematically began destroying every piece of furniture in her apartment. Wielding splintered pieces of wood, she staggered after her petrified servants and severed the carotid artery of one woman, who didn't run away fast enough causing her to slowly bleed to death. She broke the arm of another servant, who fled screaming from the harem to the infirmary for aid. When she could find nothing else to destroy, the disgraced Baskadine took a bottle of Arak from her pantry's shelves and stumbled to her bath, where she drank until she passed out.

When word of the mayhem reached the Kizlar Agasi, he strode into her apartments to witness the destruction for himself. As he stood amidst the blood-spattered debris, his expression of disgust gradually changed to one of relief. *We are rid of her at last. Nothing short of a miracle could bring her back from the Palace of Tears now. Unless some misfortune were to befall Selim, and then...*it was too horrible to contemplate. If Selim died, Mustapha would be Sultan, making Nuket Seza Valide Sultana, the most powerful woman in the whole empire.

The Kizlar Agasi left the wrecked apartment vowing to increase his protection of Selim. Even with Nuket Seza out of the way, one never knew from whence evil might arise. With so many factions vying for power and the Janissaries gaining strength daily, one simply could not be too careful.

Chapter 6

Nuket Seza's banishment had saved Nakshidil from more than bodily harm. It saved her from committing murder.

Aimée sat on a bench beneath a flowering lemon tree in her private garden. Resting her hands atop her pregnant belly, she wondered how such a drastic change had taken place. In France she had been judged by others and was found wanting. Now she had become the judge and wanted for nothing. It seemed to be an impossible shift in her reality. Had she really made the decision to end the life of another human being? Engrossed in protecting herself and her unborn child, she had never questioned her actions. Neither had anyone else. When she asked her Kutuchu Usta if it was possible to obtain an undetectable poison that might be added to food, the woman simply replied, "Yes, my lady," bringing her the poison within the hour. Perhaps beneath their refinements, the Turks truly were barbarians—and she had become one of them.

Aimée closed her eyes and inhaled the sweet fragrance of frangipani, surprised by her lack of guilt. Instead, she felt relieved to have avoided disaster. *How can I be a good Catholic and plan murder?* In the eyes of the

Church, she had already committed so many grievous sins, and continued to commit them daily—her enjoyment of sensual pleasure, her unsanctioned love affair with the Sultan, sins of thought too numerous to count, and of course, the imminent birth of her bastard child! Yet, she did not feel the least regret or remorse for any of them.

Perestu entered the garden and whispered, "Do you sleep?"

"No, just thinking. Come sit," she said patting the bench next to where she sat. "Perestu, when I was captured by the pirates, I prayed to the Holy Virgin, our Savior's mother, to save me."

"And she did. She must be a powerful god, yes?"

"Yes, my prayers were answered. I was delivered into the hands of my personal savior, Baba Mohammed Ben Osman, who brought me here. So, I was indeed truly saved."

"Lucky for you—and for me too," the young girl said, smiling broadly.

"But, if the Blessed Virgin saw fit to rescue me in that way, mustn't that mean the Church also approves?"

"I do not understand 'church,'" she said.

Aimée thought for a moment and then said, "I suppose "church" is the house of God where people gather to pray to him."

"Oh, your gods live in church?"

"Well, not really. That is, they, or rather He lived a long time ago and is dead now."

"How can dead gods punish anyone?" she asked, making Aimée laugh.

"I suppose you are right, little bird. I wish to believe in my old gods, but I am not sure if they live here."

"Surely, Allah is here with us," the young woman said opening her arms and smiling broadly. "He protects us now. No need to worry. I must go see to your dinner. Come in soon."

"I'll be in shortly," she said. As the girl left, Aimée let go of her theological musings and focused her attention once again. There still remained the question of Mustapha, the heir destined to be her son's "predecessor." Hadn't Euphemia David said that her son would ascend the throne "on the blood of his predecessor"? Mustapha was now incarcerated in the Cage, but he would become Sultan after Selim. If and when that happened, would he pose a threat to her son? Would it then fall on *her* to spill his blood, as Nuket Seza had done to all those other children? These questions truly disturbed her, causing Aimée to fear for her mortal soul. She may not be punished in *this* life, but what about the afterlife?

She plucked a fragrant frangipani blossom from the tree and held it to her nose, happy that she and her unborn child were safe at least for now. She was ignorant of the fact that the Circassian Kadine was not as fortunate. Sholay had remained in a coma for several days, in the home of Mufti Velly Zade. On the sixth day, having gone without nourishment or water, she quietly passed away. Unable to share her despair or cope with the loss, the Kadine retreated into her opium, certain that she would never again know the joy of love.

~ ~ ~

Spring quickly turned into summer, and once more the harem gardens came alive with a vivid profusion of flowers, herbs and heavily-laden fruit trees. Despite the emotional challenges, Aimée remained strong and healthy, and early on the morning of July 20, in the year 1783, she gave birth to a healthy, seven-pound baby boy. The birth of the child coaxed the Kadine from her apartments, and the site of him brought a smile to her face for the first time in months.

The Sultan named the boy Mahmud, and threw a feast in his honor for all citizens of Istanbul. Fifty thousand people filed into the First Court to receive the Sultan's gift of as much food as they could carry away, and when the evening sky darkened, a show of fireworks set the skies over the palace ablaze for more than two hours.

On the following day, the Sultan unveiled an ornate pavilion in the palace park. It was large enough to hold one hundred people and fashioned solely from spun sugar. The structure looked as if it were made of hand-blown glass, with spires, cupolas, domes and pillars. Thousands of potted tulip plants in shades of red, pink, yellow, orange and white surrounded the pavilion like a riotous lawn.

Aimée, Mahmud, the Circassian Kadine and forty handmaidens observed the festivities from another lavishly furnished pavilion alongside the Sultan's. It was the first time Aimée had been outside the seraglio in two years, and she found the celebration enthralling.

On the third night, celebrants watched a fireworks display on the ground, rather than in the sky. Miniature replicas of the palace, the Sultan's pet leopards, gazelles and bears, were constructed of wood and wrapped with fireworks. Once ignited, the models burned white, illuminating the park as brightly as daylight.

On the final day of the festivities, all the women of the harem were escorted to a screened pavilion in the park for their favorite spectator sport. Propped upon thousands of silk cushions, the enthusiastic audience watched nearly naked muscled men pitting themselves against one another. They laughed and wagered furiously on each wrestling match, betting jewelry and gold on more than just which man was strongest. Bawdy fantasies were openly shared—what they would do, in an hour or a night, with one of their favorites. When a match ended, regardless of who won, five hundred women called out their approval in loud ululations.

The celebration ended at dusk with the men's call to prayer, as the Sultan's women returned to the seraglio. The festivities honoring the birth of Mahmud lasted only four days, but would be fondly remembered by the people of Istanbul for the next hundred years.

~ ~ ~

At the age of sixty-one, Sultan Abdul Hamid felt the true joy of being a father for the first time. He marveled at his son's milky white skin that looked just like his mother's, and the dark hair and eyes that resembled his own. He was so excited by fatherhood that he discarded all of the protocols designed to keep harem women at a distance, allowing Nakshidil and the baby to visit whenever she wished. They even dined together several times a week, destroying the long-held tradition of the Sultan dining alone.

Perhaps Aimée's model of a European marriage played a part, or maybe the Sultan's adoration. Whatever the reason, their relationship exceeded that of monarch and odalisque, and caused the harem gossips to marvel at Aimée's apparent inheritance of Roxelana's legacy, the fifteenth century Russian Odalisque who had actually convinced Sultan Sulieman to legally marry her.

The Sultan, charmed by his favorite's interest in affairs of state, allowed her to regularly attend the Divan from the "Eye of the Sultan." Afterwards, Nakshidil made detailed reports to the Circassian Kadine.

The faction of the Divan that advocated westernization still comprised only the smallest number of men. But the seeds of change were being sown, and a free-thinking Frenchwoman now had the Sultan's ear—two facts her detractors were well aware of.

Nakshidil now understood that the Janissaries and their supporters were religious isolationists who continually blocked attempts to modernize the Empire. She saw the government desperately clinging to outdated traditions that separated them from the modern world. Guided by the Circassian Kadine and the Kizlar Agasi, Nakshidil intended to shape her son's perspective so that one day he might make modernization a reality and their Empire would take its rightful place.

Unaware of the forces gathering against her, the new mother settled in to an idyllic life in the harem. In early June, one month before Mahmud's first birthday, the Kizlar Agasi handed her a gift—the long-awaited letter from her cousin Rose.

~ ~ ~

My dearest cousin Aimée,

Can you imagine the shock I had to receive your letter? After word of your abduction reached us, we felt certain that you had surely met an untimely demise at the hands of your captors. It was impossible to imagine any other outcome, and I cried and cried at your terrible misfortune. It is, as you say, nothing less than a miracle that you live and prosper.

Your letter would have reached me sooner had I still been living at the address from which I last wrote you, but, alas, my position and the state of my marriage to Vicomte Beauharnais has greatly changed.

A little more than one year ago, in order to force my husband's acknowledgement of the perilous financial state into which I had fallen, I initiated legal proceedings against him. I hoped to press the Vicomte to honor his responsibility to his children and me, lest we end in the poorhouse, where we were headed. Prior to that, I had found it necessary to seek refuge in L'abbaye de Penthemont, as Vicomte Beauharnais had been completely recalcitrant in his duties. I am relieved to say that the court found in my favor, and I am presently provided for and allowed to live wherever I wish. It is all that Paris has talked about for weeks, as no woman has ever succeeded in bringing such a suit against her husband. My Aunt Désirée has leased a property outside Paris in Fontainebleau, and gen-

erously invited me and my children to live there with her.

In most aspects of my life, dear cousin, I am sorry to say that Euphemia David was mistaken, as my husband is still very much alive. Even if divorce should one day become legal, I have little hope for a second marriage, as I have two children and very little means of support.

I am filled with happiness at your positive outcome. How strange to imagine the woman you have become—the wife of a Sultan! No doubt, by the time this letter reaches you, a mother as well. Did you ever for one moment actually believe the old witch's predictions that you should find happiness in a seraglio on the other side of the world? How we reveled in the prospect of becoming queens—and so you have. As for me, any chance I may have had has surely passed. I have come to accept my circumstance and feel fortunate to have a lovely place to live with a doting Auntie and two darling children whom I adore. Although, Vicomte Beauharnais has petitioned to take our son, Eugène, into his care in September, when the boy turns five. I am doing all in my power to prevent this, but fear the courts may find in his favor, as he is legally the father, with more rights to his son than I. Hortense turns three next month, and although it would ease my financial burden were she my only child, I pray to keep my son with me.

As regards news of our families on Martinique, my parents have had a difficult time, and still struggle to make a success of the plantation. Father came to Paris last year in an attempt to re-establish himself, but did not succeed, and returned home just last month. I am sorry to say that Uncle Jean-Louis passed on last December, but Aunt Lavinia remains in good health, now residing in Fort-Royal. I posted letters to her and Aunt Sophie reporting on your good fortune.

Please write me soon and tell more of your life and news of your child.

I remain as ever,

Your loving cousin,

Rose

After finishing the letter, Nakshidil held it in her hands for several minutes, and then read it again. It had been a long time since she had thought of herself as Aimée. She heard her cousin's voice in each word, and her heart ached with the news of her struggles and misfortunes. It was hard to imagine her stoic Uncle Jean-Louis dead. She closed her eyes and tried to picture Rose's face. Scenes played across her mind of herself and Rose at the beach, chasing each other with long seaweed whips, and Rose's profile as she sat on the dirt floor of Euphemia David's hut, listening raptly to the old woman's prediction of two queens. Now Rose was as far as one could get from being royalty, having narrowly avoided destitution. But try as she might, she could not imagine Rose either poor or helpless. *She had such strength of will. I always wished to be more like her.*

On an impulse, she decided to share the letter with the Circassian Kadine. They had dispensed long ago with the formalities usually observed when visiting, and simply appeared at each other's apartments, unannounced, whenever they wished. However, on this particular day, when Nakshidil entered the Kadine's apartment, she was shocked to encounter another guest—a handsome young man who almost dropped his coffee cup when she entered.

The Kadine laughed. "Nakshidil, may I present my son, Selim."

Nakshidil bowed deeply to the Sultan's nephew and heir to the throne, and then suddenly realized that her face was not covered. She turned to the Kadine in panic.

"No one need know," the Kadine said with a dismissive wave of her hand. "Were we in France, you would be the Sultan's wife and Selim would be your nephew, no?"

The sultan's favorite looked directly into the young man's dark, almond-shaped eyes and smiled. His fine-looking face softened into a shy smile that revealed his resemblance to his mother—the large, sensual mouth and strong jaw line.

Nakshidil felt herself blush. Not only was Selim the first young man she had seen in over three years, he was so handsome. She knew from conversations with the Kadine that he was barely two years older than she. Her heart pounded in her ears.

"I am very pleased to meet you, my lord," she said, executing a curtsy.

Selim maintained his composure, despite the fact that he had seen so few uncovered women's faces since he was twelve. He had never seen anyone who looked like this one. "My mother has spoken of you often. I hoped that we might meet one day."

Nakshidil felt the letter in her hand and remembered the purpose of her visit. "Forgive my intrusion. I did not know that you were engaged, Mihrisah, or would not have interrupted. I have had a letter from abroad that I wished to share with you..." Her voice trailed off as she gingerly revealed the letter she held.

"From abroad?" the Kadine asked incredulously.

"Yes, from France."

"How extraordinary. Well then you must join us. Please sit. Selim has a great interest in foreign governments. Perhaps you might speak to him of such things."

Nakshidil reclined on a divan adjacent to the Kadine's. "Thank you, but this letter makes no mention of politics. It is from my cousin, Rose. We grew up together on Martinique, and she is now in France. I am sure..." she hesitated, unsure of how to refer to the young man, "your son would find nothing of interest or value within its contents."

She hastily tucked the letter into her girdle pocket. "But I would gladly share my very limited knowledge of such matters, with..."

Sensing her quandary, the young man said, "Please call me Selim. I am anxious to bring the modern practices of other countries to our empire. Were you Queen of France, how would you address the throne's successor?"

She thought for a moment. "If I were Marie Antoinette, I imagine I would call my son by his Christian name, his first name. But were I the dauphine's aunt, I would address him as 'your grace.'"

"And if you were not a queen, and I were not the heir?"

Her heart pounded louder in her ears. "Had we just been introduced, I would call you Monsieur and your surname, last name, rather than your first."

"Then I should like to be called '*Monsieur* Selim' as a compromise."

She smiled shyly and nodded. "Of course, Monsieur Selim."

For a moment, she lost track of everything she had learned and practiced for the past two years: her surroundings, her position, Turkish protocol. She became an ordinary young woman making conversation with a young man—a young man who made her palms sweat and the blood rise to her cheeks.

"Monsieur Selim," she said, feeling his name in her mouth like lavender serbet, "I would be honored to tell you all that I know, although I fear it may be too little to satisfy your thirst."

"A drop of water when one is parched is better than none at all, yes?"

"I see that you are already a statesman," she said.

"I have had an excellent tutor," he said, indicating his mother. "And now, perhaps I shall have another."

The suggestion seemed to hold infinite possibilities...dangerous possibilities. Rather than titillate, Selim's words had a sobering effect upon her. Although her expression did not betray her fear, her inner voice said, *No. This must not happen. My life and the life of my son depend upon my good judgment.*

"Perhaps, Monsieur. But now I must excuse myself. We will discuss my cousin's letter another time, Mihrisah."

Nakshidil curtsied. "I have enjoyed meeting you, Monsieur Selim. Goodbye."

Selim's eyes remained fixed on the door that the exotic young woman had passed through as if she might reappear. His mother watched him intently. "I think it is time for you to choose a concubine, Selim."

"Yes, Mother. I believe you are correct."

Chapter 7

Selim resembled both of his parents equally: his mother's oval face and wide, sensual mouth; his father's dark auburn hair, aquiline nose and exotic, brown almond eyes. He was tall and thin, with a delicate, almost feminine appearance, the result of his childhood brush with death at the hand of Nuket Seza. The poison had left his body weak and prone to sickness, and possibly given rise to his soft, poetic soul. But his fey physical appearance did not hamper his ability to ride or wield a sword as well as any man, and he possessed a highly intelligent and facile mind with an unquenchable thirst for life. His curiosity and excitement were infectious, and when he spoke, he transported his listeners into a world of wonder and possibility. Selim was a man who found all aspects of life infinitely interesting, living as if the days were not long enough to learn, absorb, understand and appreciate everything life offered. He shunned sleep lest he miss something of interest or importance. There was nothing he found uninteresting. Everything mattered and everyone had something of value to offer him.

Unlike most of his predecessors who spent their formative years incarcerated in "the Cage" without education or human contact, Selim had been well educated and lovingly nurtured. His uncle had personally overseen the boy's mastery of the Turkish *Book of Laws*, the secular bible that dictated the intricate formalities of the Turkish court: ceremonies, customs, dress and etiquette. He had also mastered the arts of calligraphy, poetry and horsemanship. His mother fueled his desire for knowledge, opening his eyes to the world outside the harem, outside of Turkey. She instilled a thirst for Western knowledge and culture, and the more he learned, the more he wished to know. In short, at the age of twenty-two, Selim possessed all the qualities he would need to rule the empire, along with a fervent wish to modernize it. He embraced change amidst a culture that had been bred to fear it. As sophisticated as the Turkish people could be, so were they equally rooted in the dogmas of their ancient past, and few recognized this as clearly as Selim.

Nakshidil represented the embodiment of Western ideals, and Selim wished that he did not find her so attractive. Had she not been his uncle's favorite, he might have allowed himself to hope for more from her in the future. But protocol, honor and respect for his uncle prevented him from acting on his desire. Consequently, he resolved to gain as much knowledge from her as he could without allowing himself to want anything more.

Selim had mastered every language spoken within the palace walls, and now wanted to learn French in preparation for the day when King Louis XVI might agree to send an ambassador to Turkey. The French king had already sent an unofficial attaché in the person of Monsieur Pierre Ruffin. However, as *"Chargé d'affaires"* he lacked the official status of Ambassador, which according to Turkish law prevented the Sultan from meeting with him. With Nakshidil's help, Selim hoped his uncle would write a letter to the French court containing such a request. Knowing his uncle's fondness for the young Frenchwoman, he felt sure that all she had to do was ask. Once the Sultan's seal enclosed the letter, Selim could meet with Monsieur Ruffin personally to put it in his hands. It seemed the perfect way to begin a dialogue with France, and Nakshidil was the key. He would not allow his personal feelings to disrupt this fortuitous opportunity.

~ ~ ~

Selim and his mother sat in her garden, drinking coffee.

"I have considered your wish for me to take a woman, Mother, and, of course, you are correct, as always. Do you have someone in mind?"

"Yes. I have been thinking of this for quite some time, speaking with young women who might be appropriate. There is one in particular. She is young and beautiful with a sweet disposition, and she even speaks a bit of French."

"French?"

"Yes. She is handmaiden to Nakshidil and although trained in the arts of an odalisque, has not been taken as one of your Uncle's. Perestu is her name."

"Very good. I think it is also a good time for *me* to

learn to speak French. Will you please arrange a meeting for me, perhaps tomorrow night?"

"Of course. I will send her to you after dinner. I think you will find her very pleasing."

Perhaps not as pleasing as her mistress, but that cannot be, he thought.

~ ~ ~

As usual, the Circassian Kadine saw farther into the future than anyone around her. Selim and Nakshidil were almost the same age, while the Sultan would most likely not live for more than another decade. When Selim became Sultan, hundreds of ambitious, cunning women would compete viciously for his attention. The Kadine saw Selim inheriting the sultanship with Nakshidil at his side, guiding him towards westernization, and Mahmud next in line. It would ruin her plans if a jealous woman, threatened by Nakshidil's special relationship with Selim, were to have a voice. Whomever Selim aligned himself with must owe allegiance to Nakshidil, and never threaten their relationship. The empire might be ruled for generations by scions the Kadine had personally influenced—scions that would guarantee Turkey's emergence into the modern world.

Meanwhile, Selim must not be tempted by his uncle's favorite. He must not cause any disruption between himself and the Sultan, or between Nakshidil and the Sultan, who was happy and pliable in her hands, exactly where the Kadine wanted him. Selim must forge a friendship with Nakshidil, but have sex with other women. Therefore, Perestu. The young girl was so devoted to her mistress that she would present no resistance in the future. After all, Nakshidil had raised her to her lofty position, and she could just as easily take it away.

~ ~ ~

A few weeks later, the Kadine arranged for Selim to "accidentally" meet Aimée again in her apartments.

"My son is anxious to know of Paris, and to learn the French language," she explained.

Consequently, Aimée spent the entire morning in preparation as if she were meeting a lover. She looked radiant in rose silk and sapphires. "Paris is wondrous, Monsieur Selim, I am happy to tell you about it, and to instruct you in French. It would please me greatly." She looked down and smoothed the folds of her caftan to hide the blush in her cheeks.

Aimée spent the next hour describing the homes she had visited in Paris, the churches and opera houses, the art, clothing and wigs. She spoke of the food and dining customs that, in her opinion, paled in comparison with those of the Turks.

"But I do miss the aperitifs, sherries, and champagne," she said.

"What are they?" he asked. "Perhaps you might instruct the cooks to prepare them for us."

Aimée laughed. "I have no idea how such things are

made. They are spirits—drinks made from fermented fruits, grapes, cherries and such. But champagne—oh my," she said wistfully. "I wish you could taste it. It bubbles in the glass."

Selim listened raptly. Sometimes he found himself lost in the blueness of her eyes, or the waves of her golden hair, completely unaware of her words or their meaning. He wondered if he might find her equally as fascinating if she spoke gibberish. He liked watching her little rosebud mouth as it formed words, especially French words. Thoughts of her occupied his mind constantly— even when he made love with Perestu. He bade the girl to be silent and closed his eyes to imagine Nakshidil.

"In Circassia," the Kadine interjected, "when I was a girl, there was a spring whose water was highly valued for its healing ability—much like the ones we have here. But that water bubbled from the ground. We collected it in clear glass urns to watch the bubbles dance."

"Yes," Nakshidil nodded enthusiastically, "Champagne bubbles do appear to dance, and sometimes, while bringing the glass to my mouth to drink, the bubbles burst and tickle my nose."

"Of course, we had strong spirits in Circassia," the Kadine added. "Made from grains and potatoes—much like the Arak we have here."

"Here?" she asked. "But spirits are forbidden."

The Kadine waved her hand dismissively. "There are spirits here—and those who drink them. Have you forgotten Nuket Seza? Remember that many of us were not born Moslem." She sipped her coffee and cocked her head thoughtfully. "You know, Naksh, it may be time for you to accept our religion. I did when Selim was born, and now Mahmud must be raised so."

"I have considered this, Mihrisah, and surely you are correct. Of course Mahmud will be Moslem, but for myself, it is difficult to deny the beliefs I still somehow hold."

"Nothing need be denied. There is no reason why your beliefs may not exist alongside those of the prophet Mohammed. Conversion does not require you to give up old beliefs, merely to adopt new ones."

"I had never considered it in that way," Aimée said.

"Tell us more of shampona," Selim said. "When is it served, and what does one wear when drinking it?"

Nakshidil smiled broadly at his naïveté and remembered how strange Turkish customs first seemed to her. "Champagne is served on many occasions, dinners and banquets, at the opera and ballet. One need not wear special attire to imbibe it, but as you mention it, people are usually dressed quite festively while drinking champagne."

Selim loved it all. Western civilization seemed so…civilized, especially their styles of clothing.

"When I am Sultan, I shall have shampona brought from France. I shall also banish turbans and caftans in favor of modern attire. Our cumbersome costumes serve no useful purpose whatsoever, and we have not progressed or moved forward in any way. We live as we have lived for centuries. No wonder the rest of the world thinks us barbaric. We think that we are strong, but we are only so in our own limited world. I want to be part of the rest of the world—to explore and learn."

"You may be surprised to learn how modern this empire is compared to others," Nakshidil said.

"In what way?" he asked.

"Well, I have not traveled the world, but we had no running water, hot or cold, either in France or on Martinique."

"How then did one bathe?" he asked incredulously.

"We bathed very little and then, one person at a time, in small copper tubs to which heated water had to be carried. And never naked."

"Clothed? What a ridiculous idea. It's no wonder it wasn't done often. But how did people stand being unclean?"

"With perfumes and powders. I am afraid they were nowhere near as effective as daily bathing. And Paris itself was quite filthy. One could smell the stench everywhere."

"I am surprised to hear such news. One would think that a country capable of building sophisticated weaponry would also be clean."

Aimée smiled. "I am unfamiliar with French weaponry, but one would suppose, sire."

Which led to the discussion of military matters. Aimée professed she knew absolutely nothing, but then she remembered the colorful illustrations from the French history books she had read in school. They depicted soldiers smartly uniformed and neatly lined up for battle. The front rows knelt with rifles poised, the back rows stood at the ready, flanked behind by soldiers on horseback.

Selim was intrigued. "That is just as my father said.

He brought a Hungarian general, who was serving in the French army, to train our troops fourteen years ago, but they refused to learn. Our soldiers continue to rely solely upon their fierceness and fervor. In battle, they careen around wildly, wielding weapons in both hands and killing whoever comes within their range. I am told that the Austrian and Russian troops, with whom we are now engaged, make an orderly advance into the chaos, methodically bringing our men down. My father's attempt to introduce Western military tactics and weapons failed because of the Janissaries' refusal to accept change of any kind."

"Please forgive my ignorance, Monsieur Selim, but, why exactly would the Janissaries rather fail than learn a new and better way?" she asked.

"I believe I can answer that best," said the Kadine. "For centuries Ottoman fighting forces were some of the fiercest on earth. Fearlessness and religious fervor rendered them undefeatable. But over the years, our enemies adopted modern methods and weapons that allowed them to defeat us. That was why Selim's father commissioned Baron de Tott to modernize our army. It was the first time a foreign advisor had been employed in this manner."

"Can you guess what the Janissaries did?" Selim asked.

Nakshidil shook her head no.

"They asked how they, as Allah's true protectors of the Faith, could accept teachings from an infidel. They reminded him that Islamic Law was perfect and irrefutable. Islam needed no improvement, and neither did they."

The Kadine added, "The Janissaries still refuse to acknowledge the loss of battles as well as wars. It is their fault our Empire is shrinking with the loss of territories. Every time anything new is introduced, they empty their cooking pots and beat on them, while thousands run amok in the city slaughtering infidels."

"My father attempted to persuade them by refusing to pay their salaries. Even so, the Janissaries continued to riot until they had piled six hundred severed heads by the Gate of Salutation."

Nakshidil's eyes widened in horror and she covered her mouth with one hand.

"They eventually conceded and spent the next two years training with European rifles fixed with bayonets but they mocked and disobeyed the Baron at every turn."

"Yes," the Kadine said. "It was a testament to his military prowess that he was not killed and beheaded."

"When the training was over, the Janissaries argued that the new methodical approach deprived them of hand-to-hand combat. If everyone stayed together and did the same thing, how could one man demonstrate his individual bravery? They refused to accept or even to grasp the concept of fighting as a unit."

"I wish that I could show you the books I read at school with all the illustrations. You would find them wondrous," Nakshidil exclaimed.

"Perhaps we might request some to be sent through Monsieur Ruffin, or your cousin who resides in France."

"What a wonderful idea. You will see not only the

beautiful illustrations, you will see the French language as it should be written, unlike that from my own ungraceful hand."

Selim wanted to tell her that he found nothing about her ungraceful, least of all her small, perfect hands, and that he secretly dreamed of communicating with her in French as their "private" language no one else could understand. Long ago, he had fallen in love with Western ideals. Now he was falling in love with a Westerner.

"I shall meet with Monsieur Ruffin and request these books," he said. "And perhaps we might also obtain some barrels of shampona."

~ ~ ~

In the privacy of her own apartments, Aimée questioned the unfamiliar emotions that engulfed her. She hated the thought of Selim and Perestu making love, naked together, laughing and whispering intimacies. She ached for wanting him. Oh, God, why did it have to be Perestu? Unaware of friend's secret longing, the young girl enthusiastically shared the intimate details of their lovemaking, Selim's sweet poetic nature, and his tenderness. Every word was like a knife in her stomach. And there was nothing she could do.

Nakshidil had seen girls who suffered the consequences of revealing themselves to men, their bodies bruised and welted from the beatings dispensed by harem guards. And what if the Sultan rejected her—turned against her? Might he also turn away from Selim? Both of them had enjoyed such favor, what would happen if they were cast out? Selim might be put into the Cage. She shuddered as a chill ran up her arms making the little hairs stand on end. Mahmud might be put into the Cage as well. How could she risk their well-being as well as her own? She hated the thought of endangering herself and those she loved, but neither could she abide the thought of giving up her time with Selim. It was a complex situation—requiring continual restraint and prudence—abilities in which Aimée was beginning to excel.

The Kadine, in whom Aimée was thankfully able to confide, had a different perspective, seeing Aimée, as she always had, as part of a larger plan.

"Your influence will reach far beyond this sultanship, Naksh—beyond that of your son and mine. I do not know how strongly you believe in fate or destiny. You were surely sent here for a purpose, and Selim is part of that. It is *kismet*, Naksh. I know that it is difficult—perhaps for both of you." She thought of her lost love, Sholay, and felt a tightening in her throat. "You are young and your feelings are strong. I know how painful that can be. You must trust in a greater purpose. I feel certain of this, and I am old enough to know that it is true."

Nakshidil felt grateful to share her innermost feelings with someone, and tried to take comfort in the older woman's words, but the longing for a man whom she could never have tore deeply at her core.

Two months after their first meeting, Selim sent word to Aimée that the Sultan had agreed to send a letter to King Louis. The letter would express the Sultan's wish for an official French ambassador in Istanbul. It would explain why Monsieur Ruffin could not be recognized as an empowered representative, or received by the Sultan. That afternoon, Selim dictated the content of the text, and Aimée wrote the letter.

~ ~ ~

The only factor the Kadine had not taken into consideration was something right under her nose, something she should have known but, in fact, knew nothing about. There was a spy in the palace—a white eunuch guard employed by the Janissaries. His employment had begun a little more than ten years earlier, when the Sultan began his reign. Paid with promises of power as well as gold, Cavus Hamza, an intelligent and crafty young man, had already gathered enough information to damage many people. But his interest did not lie in damage unless it served his purpose—putting Mustapha on the throne. It was apparent to him that the Circassian Kadine and Kizlar Agasi were the ones pulling the strings of their puppets, Selim and the Sultan. Physical attack on the Sultan was impossible, and if he eliminated the meddling black eunuch another would simply take his place. However, he had discovered the Kadine's vulnerability—she liked young women, and eventually he would find one willing to trade *anything* for her freedom.

He recently had the pleasure of punishing a young bath servant for stealing an odalisque's necklace, a job he regularly requested to break the monotony of his boring guard duty. Most of the women he punished were old and fat. This one was young and firm like a boy. As he beat her, it seemed a shame to waste the naked buttocks, marked enticingly with fresh blood from the lash. He had become rock-hard with each strike, the girl there on all fours, inviting him to enjoy her. She turned her head to look over her shoulder at him, eyes smoldering as she used one hand to move her buttock flesh apart and give him access. He liked the novelty of a woman's smooth bottom and tight ass—and she enjoyed it as well. He even asked her name. Hafise. Perhaps she was the one.

Chapter 8

The final months of the winter of 1789 were inordinately cold. Early in March, the palace furnaces burned at full blast throughout the days and nights as biting winds swept down from the North. The Sultan, weakened by a lingering cough, spent increasingly more time in his bed. He asked his gentlemen in waiting to retire from his quarters and allow him to rest. As his illness worsened, he asked Nakshidil to also cease her visits. The Kizlar Agasi kept Aimée informed of the Sultan's health on a daily basis as his condition continued to decline. When she was finally summoned to visit, Aimée was relieved, thinking his health must have begun to improve.

The Sultan greeted her from his bed, surrounded by a thick fur blanket. A dozen braziers burned to give the room warmth, and medicinal incense filled the air, making it seem heavy. Nakshidil was shocked by his visible deterioration. He looked thinner and older, his sallow complexion more yellow than usual, and for the first time, she felt the imminent possibility of his death.

He motioned her to approach and sit on the bed beside him. When he spoke, his voice had weakened to a mere whisper.

"Do not stand on ceremony, my love, I would like to feel you close to me now," he said.

She held his bony hand in her two small ones and kissed it. Her vigorous lover had suddenly become an old man.

"I have few regrets in my life," he said, "but the one that lies heaviest on my heart is that we did not meet when I was young."

She began to speak, to reassure him that his importance in her life could not be measured, but he put a finger on her lips to silence her. Tears welled up in her eyes.

"Allah does not reward the greedy, I know, but such is my regret…not to have had more time with you and my son, Mahmud."

He began to cough, the racking sound coming from deep in his chest. When the coughing subsided, he sipped a little medicinal elixir from a cup that Aimée held, then fell back onto his pillows and tried to control his ragged breathing. Nakshidil stroked his forehead that felt unusually warm and smiled at his neatly trimmed beard that, despite his illness, was still meticulously darkened.

"I am here for you, Sire. How may I serve?" she asked.

With a bony finger he pointed to a small silver box that sat on a tray near the bed. Nakshidil fetched it and he motioned her to open it. It was filled with gilded opium pills in several sizes, the largest being about the size of a small grape.

"Small one," he said. "I do not want to sleep yet."

Nakshidil chose a small gold pill and poured the Sultan a cup of cool mint tea to help wash it down.

"Shall I call your physicians or Kutuchu Usta?" she asked.

"No, my love. I wish to speak to you of something very important to me."

"Yes, my lord."

"It is difficult for me to talk, so please allow me to speak without interruption."

Nakshidil nodded to show she understood.

"I do not fear death—for myself. Before you came to me, I had lost interest in everything. Nothing had importance to me. I performed my duties as was expected, met with dignitaries and advisors. But I did not know how lonely I was until I met you and life suddenly became very different, meaningful and enjoyable." He coughed, and held up a finger so she would not interrupt. "You will never know how our time together, our conversations and your unending curiosity brought me so much happiness."

"And myself as well, my lord," she said.

"Thank you, dear one. Now, I am concerned with your future and that of my son who I pray will one day rule. As you know, my nephew Selim will assume the throne when I die. He is a good man and I have no doubt will rule wisely. But I cannot abide the thought of you being sent to the Palace of Tears. Neither can I imagine my little son, Mahmud, cruelly imprisoned as I was in the Cage. So, I have asked Selim to permit you to remain here, as I allowed his Mother, and to keep

Mahmud with you and never put him away."

Tears ran down Aimée's cheeks as she sobbed open-ly at his magnanimous gesture and at the thought of his passing. They caught in her throat as she pressed his hand to her face, and she felt the guilt of her friendship with Selim rise to her mouth like bile. She needed to tell him.

"My lord," she barely choked out the words. "My lord, I must tell you…"

He stopped her again by raising his hand for silence, and a weary smile softened his face. "No need, little one. It was *kismet* I thought it the best way to ensure that your future would be safe. You are both young and he will be a good father to Mahmud."

She could not believe the words she heard. He had known about her fondness and growing closeness with Selim. Had he arranged it? As the Sultan closed his eyes and drifted off to sleep she lay down next to him, her cheek against his, and wept. She cried for the father that she had never known, for the uncle who had adopted her when her mother died, for her first and lost love, the dashing Mr. Braugham, and for the kindly Baba Mo-hammed Ben Osman, who had given her a new life. It seemed that every man she ever loved had been taken from her, and now the one who had come to embody them all lay dying in her arms. She pressed her body closer to his and determined to not let him go. She would hold him close and pray to the Blessed Virgin Mary to spare him. She prayed more fervently than she ever had and wished for a priest to comfort her, to con-fess to, to be absolved by. Her prayers and wishes and sobs finally lulled her into exhaustion, and she fell into a fitful sleep.

She did not move from his bed throughout the night. Thanks to the opium, he slept soundly despite his difficult breathing. Shortly before dawn Nakshidil rose to discover that she was filled with a determined kind of anger that she had never known. Not wanting to wake the Sultan, she paced the room quietly to organize her thoughts. Then she summoned the palace physicians to the Sultan's apartment.

A short while later, eunuch guards ushered the doctors into an outer room where Nakshidil waited. They were a group of six men and four women whom she greeted, unveiled and reclining on the Sultan's raised, throne-like divan. She meant to present herself in the most imposing and imperious manner, hoping that by intimidation she might inspire them to try harder to heal their patient.

They bowed and salaamed. When she spoke there was a hard edge to her voice that she had never before heard.

"Why does His Majesty not improve?" she asked accusingly.

"His lungs are filled with water, my lady," the head physician explained. "We have done everything that we know how to do, but nothing seems to have the desired effect."

"Do more," she commanded. "All of you are to remain here with him and do more."

She rose from the divan and strode imperiously from the room. They bowed as she left and exchanged worried looks that showed they feared for their lives. What would the angry Kadine do to them if he died? They were physicians, not magicians. How could they postpone the inevitable? They stayed with the Sultan and spent the rest of the day consulting each other and every Kutuchu Usta in the palace for opinions and potions. They argued and philosophized as they measured and mixed and finally settled on three new elixirs to try.

Nakshidil had resolved to be with the Sultan whenever she chose. He had told her not to stand on ceremony, so she would not await his summons. She returned to his bedchamber early that afternoon and was immediately admitted. Despite the administration of one of the new elixirs she was disappointed to see that his condition had not changed. The physicians huddled in a corner of the room, conferring and hoping that she would not confront them again. Ignoring their presence, she went immediately to the Sultan's bed and held up a cup of serbet for him to see.

"Your favorite violet and musk serbet, my lord."

He smiled weakly and allowed her to hold the cup to his lips to take a small sip.

"They are the very first violets of spring, my lord, and this morning it was warm enough to walk in my garden. I could smell spring in the air, and if it is warm tomorrow we will go out into the sun together."

She chatted for several minutes as she fed him the cool drink, using her mind the whole time to will him to heal. After a few sips, he raised his hand to signal that he could drink no more, and she put the cup down.

"Rest now," she said, as she tucked the fur blanket

up under his chin and lightly placed a kiss on his fore-head.

She approached the three physicians, changing her demeanor to that of a woman in charge who was gravely disappointed by the incompetence of the men to whom she spoke.

"Well, what have you discovered?' she asked.

The eldest spoke, choosing his words carefully. "My lady, we have administered an elixir that we believe will help his majesty's breathing and may give him relief. We will also administer a second elixir later in the day that may help to relieve the fever, and we continue to consult and formulate, my lady. We will not cease, I assure you."

"The only assurance I want is that you will make his majesty well," she said coldly.

"We are endeavoring to do so, my lady. We are do-ing all that we know how, my lady. Rest assured."

"I shall not rest, and do not yet feel assured."

By the time her conversation with the doctors had ended, the Sultan had, once again, dozed off to sleep. She left, going directly to the Circassian Kadine's apart-ments, entering the garden without being announced.

The Kadine reclined in the welcome sunshine and frowned at Aimée's disheveled appearance and worried expression.

"I have spent the night with Abdul and he is gravely ill…worse than I have ever seen him, and the doctors say that he does not improve. Mihrisah, what shall we do?" She sank to her knees beside the Kadine's divan and began to sob. The Kadine stroked the top of her head lovingly.

"It is never easy to let go of someone you love, my pet. Such is life. We shall never understand."

Nakshidil looked up into the Kadine's eyes through tears and said, "He has made the most extraordinary gesture, Mihrisah. He knew all along about my friendship with Selim, and was glad of it. He has asked Selim to keep me here when he becomes Sultan...when he..." She could not bring herself to utter the word 'dies.' "And Mahmud will not be put into the Cage."

"Oh, Selim would never put Mahmud into the Cage, Naksh, he adores the boy. And never would he send *you* away. But it is good to have Abdul's blessings in this. He is a very wise man, indeed and a good one."

"What shall I do?" Nakshidil asked.

"Whatever you can to make the time that he has left as comfortable as possible. Is he in pain?"

"The coughing pains him and breathing is difficult, but he is so frail and weak. It pains *me* to see him so."

"Stay close to him, little one. That is all you can do."

~ ~ ~

The next day the sun shone brightly and Nakshidil arranged to have the Sultan carried out into his gardens. A large divan had been prepared for him and when he was settled, Aimée dismissed his eunuchs so that they could sit together privately. His energy had improved slightly, but in the daylight his coloring looked even worse.

"I thought that you might like to visit with your son today, Sire. Would you like that?"

"I am always happy to see Mahmud."

She summoned one of the eunuchs, asking him to fetch Mahmud, and a few minutes later the little boy came running into the garden carrying a wooden puppet. He was almost six years old and already looked as if he might be tall and lean when he grew up.

"Look what Mihrisah has given me!" he shouted as he held up the puppet for his mother to see. She examined it carefully, admiring its detail and beautiful clothes. As Mahmud's attention shifted to his father, it changed from smiling excitement to confusion. His little brows knit together in worried concern at the unfamiliar-looking, wizened figure. He sidled up to his mother, never averting his gaze from the man on the divan, as if he did not trust the image his eyes saw.

"What's wrong with Father?" he asked.

"Father does not feel well, Mahmud. He will feel much better when he has had some rest in the sunshine. Go and show him your new puppet."

The boy slowly approached the divan and held the puppet up for his father to see. The Sultan reached out his hand to lightly touch the toy, and smiled weakly at Mahmud. "What is his name?" he asked.

"I do not know, Father. Mihrisah just gave him to me."

"I think that he is a very brave puppet, just like you are a very brave boy. He must have a brave name."

"Yes," the boy said. "He is brave and knows how to fight. I will know how to fight soon also."

"It is good to know how to fight, my son, but also good to know how to think and how to pray. Mohammed knew all of these things. Maybe you should name him Mohammed to remind you that you must learn how to think and pray as well as fight."

Mahmud considered this very seriously for a moment "All right, Father. He shall be Mohammed."

The Sultan laid his hand atop the boy's head and marveled at the wonder of him. His own imminent death made him even more grateful to have sired an heir in whom he could place hope for the future. Nakshidil was the greatest gift he had ever received. Mahmud would be *his* gift to the Empire.

Mahmud played in the beautiful gardens under the watchful eyes of his nursemaid and eunuchs. He ran rather than walked, and climbed halfway up the side of one of the gilded gazebos before a eunuch stopped him. The Sultan drifted in and out of sleep, and his physicians made a fuss of changing the cool compresses on his forehead and making sure that he drank his medicines. In the late afternoon, as the day began to cool, Nakshidil sent Mahmud inside and the eunuchs carried the Sultan back to his bed.

~ ~ ~

Despite everyone's efforts, prayers and wisdom, the Sultan's condition worsened during the following weeks. He was barely able to take nourishment, and grew thinner and weaker by the day. Nakshidil stayed by his side as much as she could and finally came to accept the inevitability of his passing. His breathing became so labored that she marveled at how he could breathe at all. As she lay beside him she could now plainly hear the water in his lungs bubbling with each breath.

Word of the Sultan's grave illness reached beyond the palace walls to the city, and while most citizens added the salvation of his mortal soul to their prayers, some were making other plans.

Cavus Hamza sent a messenger to the Palace of Tears with a verbal communication for Nuket Seza: "The Sultan is dying. Make yourself ready." It would not be proper for the Janissaries to act until the forty-day mourning period was over, but they must prepare to oppose Selim before his sultanship could be ratified. Another matter would need to be settled quickly as well. Tomorrow he would bring false accusation against Hafise and have her brought to him for punishment.

~ ~ ~

Nakshidil went to the Sultan's bedchamber shortly before dusk with a lavender serbet that he was unable to drink. She lay beside his frail body as he slept, her hand on his chest, barely able to feel the rise and fall of his breath. As the sun set, dark rose—colored light filtered through the latticed windows. When she was a child on Martinique, she and Rose had called those rays "God's light." She watched the light beams find their way to a silk tapestry on the opposite wall. It was a depiction of the tree of life similar to the one that had hung in her room at Baba's. Only at that time she had not known that it was one of the oldest classical Turkish themes. The rosy sunlight illuminated several of the birds and small animals that sat upon the tree's branches, and she smiled at how beauty could find a way to illuminate sorrow. Suddenly, she realized that her hand was no longer moving up and down with the Sultan's breath. She pressed lightly on his chest and whispered his name in his ear.

"Abdul?"

He made no reply.

"Abdul?" she said louder, gently shaking his still body. Then she began to scream his name and shake his lifeless body, crying uncontrollably, "Abdul, Abdul, Abdul!" until his eunuchs came and carried her from the room, still screaming his name.

There was no comforting her. She thought that she had steeled herself for this event, but now found it impossible to accept. She was able to sleep only because, without her knowledge, her Kutuchu Usta added a small dose of opium to her tea. Zahar did not leave her side, and the Circassian Kadine stopped in to check on her several times. For two days, she neither ate nor rose from her bed. Her loss encompassed all of the men she had ever loved, and she mourned each of them until she could not cry anymore. Then she asked to bathe and afterwards prepared herself for the Sultan's funeral.

To prepare the body of Sultan Abdul Hamid for burial, it was first carefully washed and then wrapped in a shroud of heavy white silk. His ears, nose and mouth were filled with cotton wool, and he was laid on his right side in a casket made of fragrant sandalwood, with his hands crossed across his breast. Before internment, the chief Ulema [scholar priest] whispered into his ear the answers to two questions he would be asked before being admitted to Paradise.

He was laid to rest with his head turned towards Mecca, alongside his forbearers beside the Hagia Sophia mosque. For the next forty days of mourning, the members of the Ulema would recite the Koran forty times a day.

The entire population of the city of Istanbul— Moslems, Christians and Jews alike—all mourned the death of Sultan Abdul Hamid. It was April of 1789, just two and one half months before Mahmud's sixth birthday, and three months before an angry mob of French men and women would storm the Bastille to begin the French Revolution.

Although a great show of sorrow was enacted, Nakshidil thought it odd that she was the only one of the Sultan's five hundred concubines who truly mourned his passing. She would also be the only one who would miss him every day for many years. During the seven years of their relationship she had matured into the woman she would be for the rest of her life, and that woman would always fondly remember her first lover.

Chapter 9

Immediately following the forty days of mourning for Sultan Abdul Hamid, the Janissaries overturned their kettles and began rioting. They accused Selim of traitorous acts despite lack of any proof, attempting to block his ascension to the throne. For more than seven hundred years, the Janissaries had doggedly adhered to a radical fundamentalist interpretation of the Koran. Selim, like his father before him, possessed what they perceived to be a dangerous desire towards modernization. They were correct in that both Selim and his father wished to keep pace with the rest of the world. The Janissaries wanted to continue fighting as they always had, despite the fact that they were no longer able to defeat their enemies by doing so. Recent losses of territories to Russia and Austria forced the government to agree with Selim and they were able to bring the rebellion to an end. However, the Janissaries' dissatisfaction had been brewing for more than three decades, and there appeared to be no way to appease them short of moving the empire backwards instead of forward.

~ ~ ~

In the Circassian Kadine's private garden, the new Sultan Selim III and the Kizlar Agasi sipped coffee and discussed the recent debacle.

"Would that we could simply kill them all," the Kizlar Agasi said.

"Wishful thinking will not solve our problem," the Kadine replied. "Despite their lack of skill in warfare, the Janissaries still serve a purpose. We cannot eliminate them before replacing them. Imagine the city without police, the army without soldiers."

"The army may as well be without soldiers," Selim said. "They lose every battle. We need a new, modern army with modern techniques and weaponry—just as father wished. And considering the havoc Janissaries regularly wreak upon the city—they do more harm than good."

"You have the power to abolish the Janissaries, Selim, but they will never acquiesce. You will need your own army to enforce it. Creating an army will take years—and I do agree that now is the time to begin," the Kadine said.

"Perhaps an informal meeting with Monsieur Ruffin might be arranged," the Kizlar Agasi suggested. "If the French agree to furnish us with armaments we could begin to create a new army *without* the Janissaries. The French King could certainly use the revenues it would bring, and we have a common enemy in Russia."

"Yes, but I am still unable to meet with him directly

to negotiate, and we would need to choose someone we fully trust in my stead," Selim said.

"Perhaps the Mufti Velly Zade," the Kizlar Agasi suggested.

"With Nakshidil acting as interpreter—hidden of course," the Kadine added.

They all considered the possibilities an alliance with France might offer, and Selim became very excited. He paced back and forth gesturing with his hands as he spoke. "It is an excellent idea. We will need French officers to train our new soldiers, just as father did. But these men will be willing students. We'll need modern weapons, guns and cannon. We will need written instructions for the weaponry. Naksh can translate all of the French into Turkish." He threw his hands up in the air, praising Allah. "We have waited too long, and it is time to move forward. In another decade a new century begins. I want the Empire to enter the nineteenth century with the rest of the world, not straggling along behind it, or worse, beaten into dust and left behind. Mother, you are correct as always. Bayazid, make the arrangements as quickly as possible."

The following week Pierre Ruffin met with the Mufti Velly Zade in a secret room of the Divan, with Nakshidil acting as translator from behind a pierced screen. Ruffin was intrigued to finally be in the presence of the Frenchwoman who, if rumors were correct, was quickly becoming the power behind the throne. But protocol forbade him from addressing her directly as well as from seeing her. He hoped that one day an opportunity might present itself. At the moment, he was happy to agree to petition King Louis to furnish the Ottomans with the manpower and weaponry they requested. He would also again petition the King to either appoint an official ambassador to Turkey or provide him with the credential.

~ ~ ~

As that meeting was taking place, the Circassian Kadine reclined on a divan in her room of state, where she listened to and arbitrated women's formal complaints against one another. On this morning, a young bath servant stood before her. She was olive-skinned and slim hipped like a boy, with long, straight black hair and piercing black eyes. She held her head high and proud, her back erect in a defiant manner, steeled against a hostile world.

The Kadine was careful to conceal her shock, because the young girl bore a striking resemblance to Sholay.

The Baskatibe, who had brought the girl before her, said, "My lady, this girl has stolen jewelry on three occasions."

"Only once," the girl snapped back angrily.

"Quiet!" the Baskatibe commanded. "She admits to only one theft, my lady, and claims that someone made it *appear* she was responsible for the other two."

The Kadine thought for a moment, and then asked, "Have you angered another woman?"

The girl looked the Kadine in the eyes and answered, "I am sure I have angered many women, my lady."

The answer made the Kadine smile. "Why is that?"

"I am accustomed to taking what I want. I chose to be a servant...to serve women rather than the Sultan. I prefer the affections of women, and do not pretend otherwise like *they* do...my lady."

"I see. So, they punish you."

"Yes, my lady." With her last words, she blushed and lowered her head, then raised her eyes and smiled.

A familiar feeling spread through the Kadine's chest—a warm, soft opening. Her smile was the same as Sholay's. Had Sholay's soul entered this girl's body to visit her?

"You may go, Hoca," the Kadine told the Baskatibe. "I will speak with this girl and resolve the problem."

"As you wish, my lady." The Baskatibe bowed and left.

The Kadine asked, "What is your name?"

"I am called Hafise, my lady."

"Hafise, perhaps we might discuss this matter further in the privacy of my apartments later this evening?"

The girl's eyes smoldered as she looked directly into the Kadine's. "That would suit me very well indeed, my lady."

"After dinner then," the Kadine said.

"Thank you, my lady," she said with a bow, and left.

~ ~ ~

The ceremonies heralding Selim's sultancy had lasted seven days. One of the many gifts the Sultan offered
was allowing women who so wished to leave the seraglio permanently. They could choose to move to the Palace of Tears or return to their families. Only forty chose
the Palace of Tears. Of the remaining four-hundred-and-
sixty women, some returned to their families to marry
men of the family's choosing, while twenty-three asked
Selim to choose husbands for them. Within a month of
Selim's ascension, only seventy-two women remained in
the seraglio, all of them young. They knew that Perestu
was now the favorite, but the Sultan was only twenty-
seven years old, and would favor many other women in
the years to come. It did not hurt that he was also handsome and kind. Consequently, seventy young women
chose to live in hope.

Nakshidil had been comforted by the long period of
mourning, and with the help of her closest friends,
Perestu, Mihrisah, and the Kizlar Agasi, had come to
terms with Abdul's death. She remained in her apartments with her son, Mahmud, and had not seen Selim
during the mourning period, or allowed herself to wish
for his company. It was a self-imposed penance made to
honor Abdul, the man who had been so good to her.

~ ~ ~

Another two weeks passed before Perestu entered
Nakshidil's apartments one evening with a message.

"Selim wishes to see you, Naksh."

Her heart jumped into her throat. "Me?" she asked dumbly.

Perestu smiled and took her hands. "Yes, you."

"Now?" she asked.

Perestu laughed. "Yes, now, my lady."

"But, I am not prepared or properly attired," she protested.

"My lady, you are not an odalisque traveling down the golden path for a night of pleasure. Your friend Selim simply wishes to see you."

Aimée laughed nervously. "Of course, you are right, Perestu. How silly of me." She squeezed the girl's hands and stood up. "I shall go right away," she said, kissing the young woman on the forehead and leaving her rooms.

Her heart pounded in her chest with every step along the hallway to the Sultan's apartments, a path that she had walked daily for seven years. This was how her heart had pounded the first time she made the journey, with the Kizlar Agasi trailing closely behind and the Kadine's diamond belt around her hips. Everything was different now. She was a widow, living in the palace with autonomy, at no one's beck and call. Tonight she was going to see Selim, the lover of her fantasies whom she could never possess. He probably wished to discuss some private matter of state or something concerning her new French library plans. She paused outside the ornate double doors and took a deep breath before signaling the guards to pull them open.

Sultan Selim reclined on an ornate divan. "Please, Nakshidil," he said, inviting her to make herself comfortable on an adjacent divan. "You may leave us," he told his guards.

When they were alone he said, "I am truly sorry for your loss and have faith my uncle reclines comfortably in an honored place with the blessings of Allah."

"Thank you, my lord."

There was a long silence and then he said, "I feel as if I have waited my whole life for this moment, and now I hardly know what to say."

Nakshidil held her breath.

"We live in a complex situation, Naksh."

The sound of her pet name in his mouth made her blush.

"I had thought of meeting with the wise men of the Ulema," he continued, "to seek their advice on this matter, but thought better of it. Some of them have close ties to the Janissaries, and it would be unwise to expose you and Mahmud any further, especially when you are both already considered a threat to their goals. But these are not truly the things I wished to speak of with you. It appears I am having some difficulty speaking my mind clearly."

"So uncharacteristic, my lord. Perhaps I might be of assistance?" she asked.

"Yes, you might. You can tell me if you will have me," he said bluntly.

"If I will have you?" she asked incredulously. "How is that possible, my lord? You must sire children, heirs and if *I* were to become pregnant...there would be no provision..."

"You will not," he interrupted.

She stared at him blankly, her heart beating wildly in her chest.

"I am unable to sire children, Naksh. It is one of the effects of the poison. My physicians feared it might happen, and confirmed it several years ago. No one knows except my mother, of course, and now you. It would give my detractors another weapon to use against me. It is my intention to make your son, Mahmud, my chosen heir. Although I am not yet certain of exactly how to manage that. I suppose I hope the situation will somehow take care of itself. The thought of Mustapha on the throne would be certain disaster."

The information hung in the air like the aftermath of an explosion. Nakshidil's mind was going in too many directions at once for her to think clearly. *My son will be the undisputed heir*, she thought. *Selim will kill Mustapha.* The thought brought her to her feet. "This is terrible news and wonderful news. My lord, Selim." She knelt before him looking into his eyes and said quietly, "I would have you and only you until the day God takes me from this life."

He raised her to her feet and gently wrapped her in his arms. "In all the knowledge I have acquired, there were no lessons on how love might feel. I imagined it would feel different than anything else in the world; that I would know clearly if I ever had the good fortune to experience it. The first moment I saw you, Naksh, seven years ago, I felt something like a tiny flame igniting in the very center of my body." He took one of her hands and placed it on his heart. "Can you feel the heat of that little flame?" he asked.

She took his hand and placed it over her own heart. "Can you feel mine?"

"You are shaking," he said.

"Yes, my lord, I am shaking with desire. But wait," she said pulling back from him. She composed herself by regulating her breathing and smoothing the folds of her kaftan. "I think you should sit, my lord. There," she said, indicating the divan she had been sitting on. He looked at her curiously, slowly walking to the divan, where he began to recline.

"Not like that," she said gently. "I want you to sit on the edge, like this." She demonstrated, then got back up. As Selim sat, she stood in front of him and placed her hands on his shoulders. "I am not a woman of your harem, and have no intention of being treated as one." She spoke very sweetly and with a slight smile on her face. "Therefore, Selim, it is my wish to command you." His brow furrowed. "Would you not enjoy that, Selim?" she asked.

"I do not know, but I think I should enjoy anything you so desire."

"Good. So shall I. And now I think you should remove your robe and then open your trousers." She knelt before him. "I wish to see your manhood, and if it pleases me, I'll take it in my mouth."

He was almost too excited to unfasten his clothes, but did as she bade, freeing himself, already fully erect. "Naksh," he whispered.

"I am not Nakshidil, Selim, and you may not call me by that name. Not here when we are alone like this." She wrapped one hand around his member and looked up into his eyes. "You…and only you, will call me Aimée."

She took him in her mouth, licking and sucking expertly, then lifted her robes and straddled him where he sat, riding him slowly until she screamed with pleasure.

Chapter 10

The next morning Nakshidil woke early. She stretched beneath the linen coverlet and grinned, rolling over to hide her face in her pillow. She had been with Selim. Holy Mother of God, she had truly made love with Selim! And what had she done to him? It was not a dream, not a fantasy. He was huge and hard, pulling her down to drive himself deeper into her real flesh. Oh Selim, at last, Selim. She squeezed her legs tightly together and squealed into her pillow with delight. She was ecstatic, had never felt happier. She could not wait to tell Mihrisah. The Kadine had been right, as always. Patience and *kismet* worked perfectly together.

She almost jumped from her divan, splashed her face with fragrant water, and allowed Zahar to comb out her hair. Then, she donned a linen caftan and walked as fast as she could without running to the Kadine's apartments.

It was still very early, and a servant informed her that the Kadine had not yet risen.

"I shall wake her very gently," Nakshidil assured the woman with a giggle. "She will be very happy to see me this morning."

Nakshidil quietly opened the door to the Kadine's

sleeping area. She could see her friend's tousled black hair strewn across her pillow, a naked arm lying over the coverlet.

"Mihrisah," she whispered. "Wake up, Mihrisah. I have wonderful news," she said in a small, singsong voice. She gently placed her hand on the exposed naked arm, and then jumped back in shock with a scream stuck in her throat. "Mihrisah," she yelled.

Three servants ran into the room and saw Nakshidil standing against the wall with her hands covering her mouth. They rushed to the Kadine's bed and turned her cold body over. Her lifeless eyes stared at the ceiling.

Moments later, the Kizlar Agasi arrived and the distraught servants instantly identified Hafise as the visitor who had been with the Kadine the previous night. They told him she had arrived at the Kadine's invitation shortly after dinner, and left quietly, signaling them that the Kadine was asleep, just before dawn. All of the harem women and guards knew the wretched girl, and a search began immediately. The guards questioned everyone. Many were intimidated and threatened, but it yielded no information beyond the fact that the girl had been with the Kadine the previous night and not returned to her sleeping quarters. Hafise had vanished.

Cavus Hamza had not been on duty that night, so he was not even questioned, and the girl's method of escape was never discovered.

In fact, it had been quite simple. Hafise arrived at the Kadine's apartment wearing a long cloak that covered her from head to toe. As she entered and the Kadine dismissed her servants, she removed the cloak to reveal the costume she wore. She was dressed like a Tressed Halberdier, one of the young boys who delivered wood to the harem. The Kadine laughed at the clever masquerade, delighted by the girl's sense of humor.

"Do I not look like a young boy?" Hafise seductively asked.

"A beautiful young boy," the Kadine replied, as she carefully removed the headdress and wig that almost completely concealed the girl's face. She was surprised to see that the girl had cut off all her hair. "Oh, you had such lovely hair. Promise me you'll grow it back. You make a fetching boy, but I prefer you as a girl," the Kadine said, gently caressing her face with one hand. She unfastened the ties of the costume's blouse and slipped it off the girl's shoulders to reveal her small naked breasts, the nipples rouged a pale red. "With perfect little breasts, rouged for my arousal I see," she said.

"With special honeyed rouge, my lady. For your enjoyment."

"They need no enhancement for my taste, Hafise. The next time, you may leave them naked. But how could I not sample your delicious presentation?" she asked, taking one of the erect nipples into her mouth and sucking off the delicate sweetness.

Hafise arched her back and gently cupped the back of the Kadine's head to hold her mouth to her breast. "Oh, please," she whispered passionately, "kiss the other too." While the Kadine hungrily suckled the second breast, Hafise quickly removed the costume's trousers. When both breasts had been licked clean, Hafise smiled and dropped to her knees, opening her legs wide. She arched her back, resting the back of her head on the floor, and spread her nether lips with her hands, then whispered hoarsely, "Now this, my lady, please, I beg of you...taste this for me."

The Kadine removed her caftan and crawled between the girl's legs, then lifted her small buttocks up to bring her sex to her mouth. "More honey? You need it not." She licked every drop of tinted sweetness, and then began to lightly suck the little pink plum, already swollen and throbbing.

Hafise moaned with pleasure and thrust her hips rhythmically. "Oh, please, yes, don't stop, don't," she begged, thrusting her hips harder until she gasped with a final release, her whole body shaking as waves of pleasure coursed through her. When the contractions ceased and her breathing settled, she stood and held her hand out to the Kadine. "My lady," she said indicating the divan. "Please allow me."

The Kadine rose and walked to the divan with a slight stumble. "I feel a bit dizzy," she said holding her brow.

"You must have stood up too fast, my lady. Lie down for me now, and let me pleasure you."

The Kadine lay back and closed her eyes. Her head lolled to one side on the pillow as if she were drunk.

"How beautiful you are," Hafise said. "The most beautiful woman I have ever seen," she said, kissing the Kadine's breasts. "It is a pity I cannot stay with you." She kissed her belly and moved slowly downwards to the nether lips. "So beautiful." She ran her tongue lightly along the inner line of one of the lips, then probed it gently inward, finding the entrance and using her tongue to lightly thrust in rhythmically.

The Kadine moaned and tried to speak but instead mumbled something unintelligible.

"That's right," Hafise said. "Just relax and go to sleep." She moved up to lie next to the Kadine and moistened her middle finger to insert it in the Kadine's vagina. Moving her finger slowly in and out, she used her other hand to brush the long dark curls from her face. "I thought about telling you instead of killing you, but my freedom is dearer to me than any lover might ever be. And I will not only be free, I will be very, very rich. I am sorry we did not meet in a different place, but I must leave now, my beauty, and no one will ever know where I have gone. The poisoned honey rouge will give you a peaceful death."

She kissed the Kadine's lips, then stood up and carefully searched the apartment until she found the famed royal jewelry. Wrapping the ropes of diamonds around her waist and securing other precious items in hidden pockets in her trousers, she donned the costume and the cloak, then checked her reflection in the dressing mirror. When she took off the cloak, no one would ever think she was anything other than a Tressed Halberdier.

As she left the Kadine's apartments, she put her finger to her lips, signaling the guards that the Kadine still slept. She ducked into the private kitchen, which was deserted at that hour. Once inside, she removed the cloak, folded it and stuffed it behind a stack of wooden crates in a corner. She picked up an empty firewood box and exited the kitchen through the service door used by the Tressed Halberdiers to walk out of the harem.

Her boyish figure had not betrayed her true identity beneath the costume, and the long side curls obscured her face. No one took any notice of a boy walking home from work.

~ ~ ~

Once again, Nakshidil had lost her closest friend, her only confidant, her mentor and benefactor and the mother of her beloved. Once again, she felt alone in the world. Underneath her sadness was the familiar fear that she and Mahmud were in danger. No one knew for certain why Mihrisah had been killed. Many of her jewels had been stolen, but Nakshidil was not certain it had simply been an act of greed. The Baskatibe, who knew the cold and calculating Hafise well, was sure that was the case. But, how had the girl escaped, and who had been her accomplice in the Palace? Nakshidil would need to be on guard again, to increase her protection of Mahmud. She had become far too comfortable in her daily routine, too trusting. She had forgotten the danger that lurked beneath the Palace's opulent surface, and vowed never to forget again.

~ ~ ~

His mother's death solidified Selim's resolve to rid the empire of the treacherous Janissaries. In his mind, there was no doubt it had been a warning, and he was determined not to heed it. The wars with Russia and Austria were presently being lost due to their antiquated fighting techniques and weapons. He resolved to put his mother's plans into motion with the support of the allies she had carefully created: the Kizlar Agasi, the influential Mufti Velly Zade, the Grand Vizier Koca Usef Pasha and those who supported his cause within the Divan. A new army and navy would be created, and for the latter, he would raise Koca Usef Pasha to the position of Grand Admiral. Nakshidil's benefactor, Baba Mohammed Ben Osman, would add his ships and men. He would ready himself for war with the Janissaries. A letter from King Louis confirmed France's willingness to grant his request. It read:

"We have sent from our court to Constantinople officers of artillery to give Muslims demonstrations and examples of all aspects of the art of war, and we are maintaining them so long as their presence is judged necessary."

He had everything he needed to make his and his parent's dream a reality. The Empire was going to move forward.

~ ~ ~

Nakshidil was still in mourning for her friend Mihrisah, when Rose's letter arrived.

August 23, 1789

> *My dearest cousin Aimée,*
> *I write you from Trois Islets Plantation, where I have*

been since April. It is so wonderful to be home again. My darling Hortense is with me, and being made such a fuss over by everyone. Sadly, my son, Eugène, is not. The courts upheld my husband's petition to take Eugène into his custody, so he remains in France, where he will be trained as a soldier. Only eight years old, and already he is learning how to fight and kill.

I do not know if word of the unrest in France has reached you. When I sailed for home, there had been some small skirmishes and several riots. In July, an angry mob wishing to overthrow the monarchy stormed the Bastille and has now formed an illegal government. Lieutenant Beauharnais denounced his aristocratic privileges to join the revolutionary rabble, who have made him a "deputy of the new regime," whatever that means. At least he has not been hanged or imprisoned like so many of our friends. The revolutionaries call themselves the "people's national assembly." Poor King Louis.

I plan to remain on Martinique until France comes to its senses and returns to normal. However, the unrest seems to have spread to Martinique as well, in the form of discontent amongst the slaves. Why do people suddenly seem to be so unhappy with their lots in life? I am grateful for my darling Hortense, but even she is unhappy here, missing the gay, cosmopolitan diversions of Paris.

Are you still enthralled with your new life, and what of your child?

Aunt Lavinia still resides in Fort-Royal. My parents are getting on and their struggles have taken a toll on them. The plantation is failing more than ever, now that the slaves have become so taciturn and unruly. Father agrees that some type of compromise must be made, but no one has yet come forward with an acceptable plan. To simply free them would throw us all into ruin.

By the time this letter reaches you, I may have already returned to France, as I must first send this to Monsieur Ruffin's office in Paris to be forwarded to you through him. Write to me in care of Monsieur Ruffin, as he will know where to forward your letters. I wish we were not so very far apart.

I send you fond hugs and kisses.

Your loving cousin,

Rose

Nakshidil was excited to receive a letter from Rose, but found the news about France confusing and disturbing. She immediately summoned the Kizlar Agasi and translated the pertinent information for him.

"What does this mean?" she asked.

"When people wish to overthrow a king, it is usually because he has become weak. Monsieur Ruffin has always said that the French king is extremely young and inexperienced. It is also common knowledge that the king's financial support of the war between England and the Americas has drained the country's coffers. Regardless of the reason, it is a dangerous situation." He thought for a moment. "However, there is always the possibility that a new government may be more responsive to us. Apart from the men he agreed to send, the King has still not appointed an ambassador. I will bring this information to the Sultan immediately. We must arrange another informal audience with Monsieur Ruffin. He will have more information. Thank you, Naksh. I will advise you of the time of the meeting."

August 24, 1789

> *My dearest cousin Rose,*
>
> *I received your letter yesterday with bittersweet emotions—so happy to hear from you yet so disturbed by your news of France. The information had not yet reached us, and I am not quite sure what to make of it. It is not difficult to imagine people who wish to overthrow their own king. We harbor a similar faction here, the Janissaries. They refuse all change within the empire and, largely because of them, it has remained unchanged for seven hundred years. What do the Parisian revolutionaries desire? Surely, they do not resist progress, as Paris is so very modern. Why are they displeased with their king?*
>
> *My son, Mahmud, is now six years old, intelligent and serious like his father, strikingly handsome with his father's black hair and my blue eyes. He is my joy, as I know you understand, essential as the air I breathe.*
>
> *My husband, Sultan Abdul Hamid, passed away four months ago following a long illness. We miss him dearly.*

She paused for a moment debating whether to mention Selim. She longed to reveal her affection for the young man to her cousin, but felt it inappropriate to describe her new love in the same letter that revealed her husband's death.

> *I also recently lost my closest friend, Mihrisah, wife of the former Sultan, and mother of the current Sultan, Selim. She befriended me when I entered the harem, taught me more than I can ever explain, and saved my life and that of my son on more than one occasion. Oh, Rose, you cannot possibly imagine the degree to which my life has changed. We would need to talk for weeks to catch up. How I wish we could do exactly*

that. I miss Mihrisah and Abdul so terribly. It seems that everyone I love is taken from me, even you, my dear cousin, who reach out to me from so far away.

Enough talk of death and sadness. Now, I wish to tell you of other things. King Louis has agreed to send us French military advisors to modernize our army, and in preparation, I am teaching Sultan Selim to speak French. Towards this purpose, he wishes to bring tutors and books from France, for himself and Mahmud. Monsieur Ruffin has been charged with finding the appropriate people, and if you know of anyone, please let him know. I have suggested we import some of the comforts I miss as well—chairs and tables, chandeliers, sherry and champagne. The Sultan is very excited to taste champagne, as nothing like it exists here.

Please give my regards and best wishes to everyone at home, and write soon with news of France. Have our aunts and uncles in Paris also renounced their privilege? Let me know when you return and establish a permanent residence.

Your loving cousin,
Aimée

Chapter 11

February, 1792

Mahmud ran excitedly into the Sultan's garden, waving a small sword. "Uncle Selim, Uncle Selim! May I show you what Captain Bertrand just taught me?" Although they were technically cousins, Nakshidil had encouraged the use of the term "uncle" after Mahmud's father died.

Selim sat at a small Rococo-style writing table, recently arrived from France. He ceased writing and pushed his chair away from the table. "Of course, Mahmud. Just try not to kill any unarmed plants or trees."

Selim swelled with pride when he observed the nine-year-old boy who was already taller than his mother. His astonishing blue eyes widened with excitement as he held the sword hilt with both hands and took a classic fighting stance. The expression on his face changed from a smile to a frown of focused concentration. Raising the sword high over his head, he brought it down fast, slashing from right to left, then left to right, as he simultaneously moved forward, mowing down lines of invisible attackers.

He stopped and looked to his uncle for approval.

"Quite impressive, young man," Selim said. "I doubt that any of your opponents would still be standing."

"*Oui*," the boy automatically answered in French. "They would all be dead, sir."

"And who is the enemy today?" Selim inquired.

"Russians," Mahmud replied. "On horseback."

"I see. Well, in that case, you may want to slash a bit higher," Selim advised with a smile. "You may not want to display your new skill to your mother. Captain Bertrand is here to train our new army, not the royal heir who is supposed to be studying."

"I finished my studies and Mother is playing her harpsichord. Captain Bertrand saw me in the courtyard with my sword and..." He trailed off.

"You will be a fine swordsman, Mahmud. But a Sultan must also be a scholar."

"Father told me I should also know God and the Prophet," the boy replied.

"Yes, that too, Mahmud. A Sultan must know many things and be many things."

Mahmud was everything a royal heir should be—intelligent and kind, with a strong innate sense of morality. Unfortunately, Mustapha was next in line to inherit and Selim continued to search for a legal way to promote Mahmud's ascendance in his stead. There was no doubt Mustapha would quickly throw the empire into chaos and take great delight in doing so. At thirteen years of age, he was emotionally unstable, with a violent and sadistic nature, while his mother was a pawn of the Janissaries. Mahmud would be safe as long as Mustapha remained in the Cage. However, if the deranged young man were put in a position of power, hundreds, perhaps thousands of heads would literally roll. It was a quandary that occupied Selim's thoughts often, and one he could not solve. Murder was the only way to prevent Mustapha from becoming Sultan, and Selim found that difficult to initiate or condone. The only execution he had ordered thus far was that of the Grand Vizier Hassan, Commander-in-Chief during the failed wars with Austria and Russia.

During the first year of his reign, the army had suffered defeat at the hands of the Austrians. The following year, the army of Catherine the Great, Empress of Russia, attacked the fortress of Ismail, forty miles from the Black Sea, capturing the city and brutally slaughtering thirty-four thousand Turkish subjects. Selim blamed the defeats on the outdated fighting tactics of the Ottoman army that consisted solely of Janissaries, and blamed Hassan for being unable to persuade his troops to modernize. Consequently, Selim became even more committed to creating his new army.

To that goal, the Sultan sent lists to Paris of the positions he wished to fill. Soon after, French artillery and naval officers arrived in Istanbul with modern rifles fixed with bayonets, cannons and cannon balls, and engineers with plans for a cannon foundry to be built on the shore of the Bosporus. The Turkish recruits who volunteered attended a new military school in the Levend Ciftlik, where they trained in European military tactics and learned to speak French. It was mandatory for all students to learn the new language, and conversely, the French instructors learned Turkish.

However, the Janissaries remained stubbornly adverse to the teachings of infidels, refusing to accept instruction from foreign officers unless they converted to Islam. In their resistance, the Janissaries enlisted the support of the Ulema, Islamic priests and scholars, who brought the matter before the government of the Divan. Prolonged discussions on the matter ensued.

Some Ottoman officials suggested dividing responsibilities by using the Janissaries to fight wars, while creating a new militia to guard Istanbul. Others suggested bribing the Janissaries by meeting their most recent demands for pay increases and improvements in their living conditions. Finally, everyone agreed upon the latter, raising wages and enlarging the barracks while issuing new rifles with bayonets. In response, the Janissaries revolted, confirming Selim's belief that nothing would convince the Janissaries to move forward or change in any way. He was correct in his plan to create the new army.

July 1792

> *My dearest cousin Aimée,*
>
> *Can you ever forgive almost three years of silence? You cannot imagine the devastating changes that have overtaken our beloved France. I struggle to simply keep a roof above our heads and food in our mouths. The country is bankrupt, the people starving and lashing out at one another to survive. Prisons and poorhouses are overflowing, and death is every-*

where. Brothers have become enemies, and friends are now foes. My husband and son are strangers to me, distant ghosts that Hortense and I rarely see. Thank heaven for Aunt Désirée, who has given us shelter, or we would surely have perished as so many others have.

The revolutionary government has imprisoned the King and Queen at the Tuileries. They remain unharmed, yet forbidden to leave the grounds. They say King Louis has given all of our money to help the American colonies fight the English. Those clinging to, or even suspected of clinging to the old aristocracy to which we unfortunately belong are brutalized or imprisoned. "Citizens" now eagerly prove their loyalty by denouncing each other for the slightest (or imagined) occurrence. There has also been a good deal of anti-Catholic ranting. It is not safe here. Perhaps it is not safe anywhere in France.

I hesitate to write these things to you, firstly, because I can hardly believe them myself and hoped they might dissipate like an unwelcome dream, and secondly, because you are so far removed. I remember how helpless and despondent I felt when we believed you lost, and do not wish those feelings upon you now.

Do you remember Euphemia David telling us that my husband would die "as a result of troubles that would befall the land of the Franks?" We seem to be in the midst of those very troubles, and I live in mortal fear of this coming to pass—not for loss of a love we never shared, but for the small security it affords.

Please pray for my family and me and know that should anything happen to me, I have always remained your loving cousin,

Rose

Nakshidil held the letter in her hand and began to sob. Rose was right, she felt helpless. What could she do?

She dried her eyes, and walked down the long hall to the Sultan's quarters. Seeing her approach, one of the guards, accustomed to the Kadine's unannounced visits, stepped inside and immediately reappeared to open the doors wide for her to enter.

Selim sat at his secretary desk amending a piece of music he had been composing. Seeing the distressed expression on her face, he set down his pen and rose to greet her.

"A disturbing letter from my cousin Rose in France," she said, holding the letter out to him.

Now fluent in both spoken and written French, Selim read the letter quickly. He guided Aimée to a divan, and signaled a servant to bring coffee.

"Monsieur Ruffin has spoken to me of these things," he said. "I had not thought of how they might affect your family there. We will send gold. Perhaps she can buy her way out of these troubles, or at least out of France for a while. She must go where she will be safe." He gazed reassuringly into his lover's eyes. "We will send her the means to buy whatever she needs, my love."

"What if it does not reach her in time?" Nakshidil asked, with a pained expression.

"I will summon Monsieur Ruffin immediately and ask his advice in this matter," Selim replied. "Even the fastest ship will take more than a month to reach France." He remembered the Dey's fleet that had been moored in the bay of Istanbul for several months in anticipation of another Janissary revolt. *Perhaps Baba Ben Osman has a faster one,* he thought. At a little over sixty years of age, Baba Mohammed Ben Osman still ruled over his fleet. "I will also summon Ben Osman," Selim said aloud.

"Yes! Ask Baba for his fastest ship, please," she pleaded. "Oh, would that I could go," she added.

Selim regarded her incredulously. "Surely, you are not serious," he said.

"Oh no, Selim, just wishful. I just wish I could be with Rose when she needs someone so much."

She snuggled against Selim, who wrapped his arms around her protectively and kissed the top of her head.

"I will send the summons out immediately, Naksh. We will do all that we can. Do not fear for your cousin."

He said the words in reaction to Nakshidil's apparent distress, but without real understanding of her feelings. Selim was a child of the seraglio ignorant of the familial bonds of European families. His mother and uncle had been the only blood relatives he had ever known, and he had never fathered a child. His compassion was a testament to his deep sense of morality. And Aimée was the only person left whom he truly loved. Her unhappiness therefore became his own.

Two days later, Baba Mohammed Ben Osman's fastest ship, captained by his eldest son, sailed for France carrying a small wooden chest of gold and a letter from Aimée.

September, 1792

    My dearest cousin Rose,

    I pray this letter finds you and your family safe and well, and hope the gift I have entrusted to Monsieur Ruffin's representative helps to alleviate at least some of your suffering. I am sorry I did not think to do so sooner. But, who could have foreseen this madness? The situation you describe brings tears to my eyes and makes my stomach churn. Has all of France gone mad? Is there somewhere safe you can go? Where are Aunt Sophie and Uncle Jean-Louis?

    All is well here but I beg you to please let me know if there is any more I can do to help. You are correct regarding my feelings of helplessness but at least this is something that with the aid and good will of Sultan Selim, I can do. Please, please be safe.

    Your devoted cousin,
    Aimée

Chapter 12

Two years passed without word from Rose. When a letter finally arrived Aimée frantically tore it open, scanning its contents as fast as she could. The last paragraph read:

"You, my cousin, always so pure and god-fearing. It is difficult for me to imagine the woman you must now be to have gained the lofty position of power within the sensualist realm of the Ottomans. Has fate caused the reversal of our childhood roles and cast you as the wanton and me, the poor widow?"

With tears streaming down her face, Aimée pushed open the secret door that lead from her apartments to the Sultan's and burst into his bedchamber. Holding the pages of Rose's letter in her hand she cried, "Selim! Terrible news…from Paris."

Selim moved quickly to her, as she collapsed in his arms. She was crying too hard to continue speaking as she pushed the letter into his hands. Selim read the letter with disbelief. Rose's husband had been executed by the revolutionary government, as had both the King and Queen. Rose had been imprisoned for four months, almost dying from the inhumane conditions and lack of food. Her son was in the army, and her daughter had luckily been living with an aunt in Fontainebleau. The family estate had been confiscated and would be "redistributed" to the peasants. Aimée's gift had saved her life by allowing her to buy her way out of prison. Now, everything was gone, and Rose was destitute. The entire country continued to reel from the on-going upheavals and atrocities of the revolution.

"Her husband is dead, and the King and Queen. France is lost." Aimée sobbed. "Oh, my poor, poor Rose."

"We will send help," Selim said quietly. He began to calculate possible implications for his own Empire. Over the past four years, France had furnished him with a continual stream of officers, engineers and artillery specialists to train and work with his new troops. What might they do now, and what position would Monsieur Ruffin take? It did not bode well.

November 1794

> *My dearest cousin Rose,*
> *I cannot bear the thought of the horrors you have endured. I mourn your personal loss as well as that of France. I have entrusted Monsieur Ruffin with another package for you, along with this letter. How can these things happen in a civilized country like France? And who will rule now that they have killed the King and Queen? What will happen to the royal children, the Dauphine?*
> *Oh, my dear Rose, I am helpless being so far away, and I fear what may befall you and your children before you receive*

this letter. After receipt of your last letter, I began praying again. Know that I pray daily for your safety, and for sanity to return to France, though I am no longer sure upon whose ears my prayers may fall.

It seems pointless for me to write about myself, as nothing of any great importance is happening here. You may find it interesting that I am building a library in Istanbul, a French library. Sultan Selim and I have become quite close since my husband's death, and he acts more father than cousin to Mahmud, who adores him.

I pray that my gifts help to alleviate your situation and bring you some respite. Please write immediately to let me know that you received everything and whether you are moderately comforted or relieved. My heart aches for your loss and your troubles, my darling cousin. Would that I could do more, and let me know directly if I may.

> *Your devoted cousin,*
> *Aimée*

After finishing the letter, she dropped two handfuls of loose diamonds, rubies and sapphires into a calfskin purse. She wrapped the pouch within a blue cashmere shawl, and placed the precious bundle into a wooden box, then sealed it with wax. The Kizlar Agasi would deliver the package into the hands of Monsieur Ruffin, who would personally transport it to France for delivery to Rose. It would take six weeks for her cousin to receive the package, and another six for word of its receipt to come back to her. She would not rest peacefully until she knew that it had. *What if Rose was imprisoned again? What would happen to her children? What if she died?* The last thought doubled her over, and she sobbed as if her fear was, in fact reality. Rose was more than her closest relative. She had become her lifeline to the outside world. How small might Aimée's world become without Rose?

~ ~ ~

Selim's "Secret Army" currently consisted of sixteen hundred men who resided and trained ten miles outside of Istanbul in Levland Ciftlik. The first two hundred men had volunteered from Koca Usef Pasha's personal army of Russian and German deserters. One hundred additional young men were recruited off the city's streets and spirited away before the word could spread. French artillery officers trained the recruits in military formations, tactics, modern weaponry and the French language. They were the first Turkish soldiers to become proficient in the European style of warfare. Their uniforms, modeled after those of the French, consisted of breeches, soft, brimless blue hats like berets and red tunics. In two months' time, they would be introduced to the general populace as the "Riflemen of the Corps of Gardeners," and no one knew how the Janissaries might respond.

~ ~ ~

Pierre Ruffin returned to Istanbul from France in February of 1795 after a round-trip voyage of just three months on one of Baba's ships. He brought a letter from Rose that he delivered to Selim. The two men had been meeting on a regular basis for several years, and now sat in one of the Sultan's informal meeting rooms.

"Madame Beauharnais appears to be well recovered from her travails," Ruffin reported. "She asked that I personally convey her deepest gratitude to you."

"Thank you. I know the Valide Sultana thanks you as well. Please tell me all the news from France," Selim said.

"Unhappily, it seems that order returns only to be challenged. Royalist opposition always seems to be brewing somewhere, despite the fact that most Frenchmen seem pleased with the new government. And if our own unrest were not enough, we had to send troops into Amsterdam. There seem to be rebellions everywhere these days." He sighed heavily.

"Yes, I understand. The more reform I attempt to bring about, the more opposition I encounter. Our "New Order" has brought so much good change to the people with land reform, education, reduced taxation, and new limitations on the powers of overbearing Pashas. But some factions still resist change of any kind, good or bad."

"The Janissaries?" Ruffin asked.

"As always the Janissaries," Selim replied. "They continue to eschew our new military and naval schools, and refuse to learn French. Apparently, they would still rather die than learn from foreigners—and so they may. Hopefully, they will not take the whole Empire with them."

"How goes the rest of the empire, my lord?" Ruffin asked, hoping to discover some piece of new information about Egypt. The French still longed for a handhold in the East, and news of civil unrest there had spread to the continent. Russia had her eye on it as well. If the Turks lost possession, both empires would vie for the prize.

"Some of my other subjects also prefer to cling to the past," Selim replied. "No doubt you have heard the talk of rebellion in Arabia, Syria, Palestine and Egypt. It is fueled by religious radicals not unlike the Janissaries. They support the old ways and wish to see Mustapha in my place. They believe he would be a "manageable" Sultan because he is young. But they do not know him as I do. He is a terribly unbalanced young man, filled with anger and hatred, who enjoys seeing people suffer—actually watching people suffer physically. I've no doubt that were he Sultan, thousands of heads would roll. It would be a bloodbath."

"Let us pray you prevail, sir, with the aid of your new fighting force. I fear you may need them. If I and my country may serve you further, you have only to ask."

"Thank you, Monsieur. The French government's generosity shall not be forgotten. Your people here have become invaluable to us, despite the misfortunes of the revolution in their own country. The time will come when all of our empire will look upon France as I do and acknowledge the role she plays in our development."

Ruffin lifted his glass of champagne and extended it towards Selim. The high-pitched clinking of the crystal echoed through the domed room. *"À la santé de l'empire,"* he toasted.

"Merci, mon ami," the Sultan replied.

August 28, 1795

> *My dearest cousin Aimée,*
> *I continue to be overwhelmed by your generosity. Not only did your jewels allow me to extricate myself from poverty and avoid the poorhouse, they enabled me to move back to Paris with Hortense. It is encouraging to see the city regaining some of its old character and coming back to its senses. Recently, we held a national convention to write a new constitution for a "Liberal Republic." A central government of five men, called The Directory, is now in power, and although still in a state of flux, seems quite effective. They recently settled my husband's estate quite fairly upon the children and me. I consider it extremely fortunate that an old family friend, the Vicomte Paul de Barras, (now citizen Barras) is one of the five directors.*
> *I am sorry to tell you that Father passed away amidst the riots and chaos into which both France and Martinique were thrown. I am grateful for the time we spent together on my last visit and that he came to know his granddaughter. Mother now lives in Fort-Royal with Aunt Lavinia, and sends us a small monthly stipend from Father's estate. I cannot imagine how she will get on without Father, but perhaps she is stronger than I know.*
> *I have leased a lovely home on rue Saint-Honoré with a*

small but adequate staff of servants. Parisians appear to have settled into a somewhat comfortable rapport with one another, greatly relieved to have food on their tables and a modicum of security in our daily lives.

Social rapport has changed as well with "salons" replacing formal gatherings where citizens (as both women and men now call ourselves) discuss matters of importance rather than gossip. I am surprised to discover my interest in matters such as the making of laws and the machinations of government, which I find quite fascinating.

Our manner of dress has changed radically and is now quite simple—no more complicated undergarments, hoops, stays or wigs. The less complicated dress eliminates the need for servants to assist in dressing, you see. I much prefer it, as it reminds me of the simplicities of our youth on Martinique, although my shifts are now made of silk instead of linen. I must be getting old, cousin, as I have taken to reflecting on the happiness of my youth.

So, my dearest, my worst fear came true (as predicted), and I am a widow with two children. Hortense is twelve and Eugène already a young man of fourteen. We were just fourteen when we ran off to see Euphemia David. Speaking of that old witch, I recently met an extraordinary woman who considers herself "gifted" in a similar fashion. Her name is Marie Le Normand, and she hosts the most marvelous salons, though her "talents" do not compare with those displayed by Madame David.

Aunt Sophie and Uncle Jean-Louis have returned to their house—no doubt a testament to Sophie's distinct manner of "charms" and persuasion. Now free of the restrictive niceties of her class, Sophie has become more notorious than ever. They say she has at least three lovers in addition to her Italian who still resides in her attic! Mon dieu, I do not know how she manages it.

The last remaining Royalists, mainly Catholics backed by the English, were recently defeated in La Vendée. The Revolutionary government has supported anti-Catholic sentiments here for several years, and no one practices openly anymore or wishes to be associated. So, you see, cousin, I too am no longer sure who hears my prayers, although I am certain who answers them—it is you.

I close in gratitude, and remain as ever your devoted and loving cousin,

Rose

~ ~ ~

Perestu entered the magnificent apartments, formerly occupied by the Circassian Kadine, where Nakshidil now lived. A mature woman of twenty-seven, she was still slight of build, now resembling a sleek cat more than a small bird. Her halting Turkish had been replaced by impeccable French, which she often chose to speak over Turkish.

Noticing the letter in Nakshidil's hands, she asked, "From Rose?"

"Yes, and for once it is mostly good news. When I read her words, I can hear her voice and sense the relief...even happiness. She is much changed."

"I am glad. I know how much you care for her, and how difficult it has been for you to be so far away when she needs you."

"Thank you, Perestu." She saw the sadness on the younger woman's face and asked, "What troubles you, little bird?"

"Last night..." her voice faltered. "My moon cycle began again," she whispered and began to cry.

She lived in the constant hope of becoming pregnant, and now began to fear that its absence was her fault. She laid her head in Aimée's lap and sobbed as Aimée stroked her hair.

"Oh, Perestu, I am so very sorry. So sorry, my sweet. Have you spoken with Selim about this?"

"Oh no. I could not." Her lovely face filled with pain as she looked into her friend's eyes. "Why won't Allah give me a child, Naksh?"

"I am not sure why any God does anything. I have asked mine for many things that have not been given. But, I think you must talk with Selim about this."

Nakshidil held her sobbing friend, and resolved to speak with Selim herself. He must disclose his disability to the girl. She would never reveal the information to anyone else, and it was senseless to live with a hope that would never be fulfilled.

Neither woman could have known that Perestu's inability to conceive was also the concern of Cavus Hamza. Since Selim's ascension, the spy had paid close attention to the Sultan's assignations, watching and waiting for pregnancies and births that never took place. He carefully noted the lack of fertility within the harem and began to devise a plan to make the information public—as a topic of gossip in the Divan. After all, the Empire had never been ruled by an impotent Sultan. A respected ruler needed to be virile and prolific, to sire sons that exemplified that virility. The Quran might even speak about this anomaly. He made a mental note to ask a member of the Ulema. He had no doubt that if more people were made to see Selim's weakness, they would join with the Janissaries and overthrow him to put Mustapha on the throne. A young foolish Sultan would be easily manipulated, leaving the governing to older, wiser men like himself. With Sultan Selim gone, it would be simple to eliminate the only other pretender, Mahmud.

October 10, 1795

Dearest, dearest Rose,

What a great relief to know you and your children are finally safe—France too, one hopes. My prayers were answered the day your last letter arrived. I feared that amidst the unrest, Monsieur Ruffin might forsake his position and that I would, in turn, lose my ability to contact you. All appears to be well at last, and I am happy to say it goes just as well here.

My little Mahmud is no longer little at twelve years of age, and cares more for his true swords than he ever did his toy soldiers. Why do all boys wish to be soldiers, and why do they have no regard for death as we do? What a little man he has become.

I am excited to tell you that we now have a French printing press that produces our own French newspaper here in Istanbul. Wonderful changes have taken place since Selim became Sultan six years ago, and your new revolutionary government has been extremely generous towards us, sending soldiers to train our men in the new methods of warfare and armaments. Next spring, we begin the construction of our first foundry, under the advisement of French engineers and artisans. It will enable us to build cannon and balls to protect the city, and they are building a fortress right above the palace. It is all too exciting for words. My French library in the city was completed last year, and now contains over one thousand books—all imported of course.

I am relieved beyond description for your happiness and well-being, and wish you to know that I too am equally well. I could not tell you of my love for Selim in my last letters because it pained me to speak of my happiness when yours seemed so far away. Before my husband (as I think of him), Selim's uncle, died, he gave us his blessing and charged Selim to care well for Mahmud and me. Now our friendship has grown into love, and despite the many other women who share his affections (difficult for you to grasp, I am sure), it is quite extraordinary. I wish you could be here to see for yourself, for it is unlike anything we ever imagined—ever.

With fondest regards and kisses, your loving cousin,
Aimée

Chapter 13

Rose looked over all her dresses and carefully chose the newest and most attractive one, a dark green silk shift in the latest style. She slipped on a pair of matching satin slippers and tied a simple scarf once around her head to hold her long auburn curls in place, allowing a few curls to spill down the sides of her face and neck in a girlish manner, hoping to create the illusion of youth. Considering her reflection in the looking glass, she thought she might actually appear a bit younger than her thirty-two years. She sighed deeply. *Everyone already knows me for what I am,* she thought, *a middle-aged widow with two grown children.* Fortunately, she had no need of financial support and would happily settle for a man's companionship or...*perhaps I should just take a cadre of lovers, like Aunt Sophie did.* She adjusted the scarf in her hair and thought, *Why not a second marriage? All aspects of Madame David's predictions have come to pass thus far. Perhaps I might also be a queen.* She laughed at her distinctly un-royal reflection in the glass.

Rose thrived on the lively evenings she spent at Mlle. Le Normand's salons, the interesting discussions about government and policies with artists who cared so passionately for everything. Tonight, her friend Paul Barras said, there might be an interesting foreigner at the soirée, a military man of some sort whom he thought she might enjoy.

She was still adjusting her curls when the front door knocker sounded, and a moment later her housekeeper entered the dressing room holding a calling card in her hand. "Citizen Barras has come to call," she said.

Rose entered the parlor and extended her hand in greeting. "Monsieur Barras, how odd. I was just thinking of you when the knocker sounded."

"Madame de Beauharnais," he said, kissing the back of her hand, "It is always a pleasure to see you. I realized as I approached your house, that you might care to ride to Mademoiselle Le Normand's with me."

"Yes, of course. How thoughtful."

"And on the way, I will tell you about the gentleman I want to introduce you to this evening. I have a distinctly strong feeling about this one, Madame. I find him fascinating, and think you might as well."

They entered the waiting carriage and settled into the cozy velvet seats, sitting side by side rather than across from one another. Rose rested her hand on the inside of Monsieur Barras's thigh and looked up at him invitingly. "You are so very thoughtful, Monsieur," she said with a smile. He kissed the nape of her neck as she said, "Now you have piqued my curiosity, chérie. Tell me more of this man you find so fascinating, and tell me why you find him so."

"Well, of course you are aware of the incident at the

Tuileries ten days ago, the one everyone is now calling
13 *Vendémiaire*?"

"Of course, all of Paris knows about that."

"Then you may also know that when the angry mob
of Royalists tried to attack the Convention, it was this
young man who brought the cannon and fired grapeshot
upon the mob, clearing the streets instantly."

Rose gasped. "Yes, he has some strange foreign
name. Is he a general then?"

"No, but I immediately promoted him to the rank of
Major."

"Firing on fellow Frenchmen must have been a difficult choice to make," she said.

"For an ordinary man, perhaps, but it was his idea
and he never hesitated. I must admit, in many ways, he
is not a typical Frenchman."

"Now I am intrigued. Exactly how is he not typical?" she teased.

"He is Corsican."

"Corsican? Oh, yes. He is Italian."

"Not technically, despite the fact that everyone still
thinks Corsica to be Italian. France actually purchased
the island one year before his birth, so he is in fact a
French citizen. Although, I must say, he seems quite Italian in appearance and temperament—darkly brooding
and quite passionate."

"Hmm, that does sound intriguing. And his family
is?" she let her question rest there without completion,
as she had become accustomed to doing. No one was
supposed to care any longer about rank and aristocracy,
but, of course, the aristocracy still cared deeply.

"Of little consequence, although his father was a lawyer at King Louis's court for a few years. Fortunately, it was long before the troubles began. The father's position afforded the young man the best military schooling, during which he distinguished himself quite admirably. That is where I first encountered him—when he was just fifteen."

"And, how young is he now, Monsieur?" she asked.

"Not too young, Madame, just twenty-seven."

"Oh, *mon dieu*. Why would he care for a woman of my age?"

He smiled conspiratorially. "Because, my dear, like many an ambitious young man, he requires your position and money."

"Oh, you are a devil!" she laughed. "I see you have a plan for my future...and just when I had decided to take another lover instead of a husband."

He lifted her skirts and ran his hand up the inside of her naked thigh, bringing his face very close to hers. "What might prevent you from taking as many lovers as you wish, Madame, once you are respectably married to a man for whom I predict greatness?"

His touch made her moan softly. She closed her eyes and rested the back of her head on the seat. "What indeed?" she whispered. "Won't you be jealous?"

"There is no room for jealousy in either war or politics, and I intend to guide this young man in both. One can never acquire too many well-placed friends," he said, taking her hand and placing it on his erection. "And he will need to travel with the army for most of the year."

"Oh, you truly are a devil, *cherie!* I doubt I shall like him as much as you. What is his name again?"

"Probably too Italian for a man with his ambitions, Napoleone Buonaparte."

"*Mon dieu.* He sounds more like a *Signore* than a *Monsieur.* Well, what's in a name? as *Monsieur* Shakespeare said."

December 17, 1795

My dearest cousin Aimée,

This may be the happiest Christmas I shall ever have. My dear friend Paul Barras, whom I mentioned in my last letter, recently introduced me (exactly two months ago today) to the most intriguing young man, who has just proposed marriage to me! His name is General Napoleone Buonaparte, and he is of Corsican birth. He is hailed as a hero in Paris, for it was he who finally put an end to the Royalist revolts on 13 Vendé-miaire (the first month in our new Republican calendar) and brought hope for the end of the revolution. Monsieur Barras recently appointed him to lead our army fighting foreign wars. He is unlike my departed husband in every way—short of stature and exotic in his dark, swarthy looks, of a serious na-ture and quite passionate.

So, my dearest dear, at last it has come to pass. My second marriage to a man six years my junior and with much prom-ise. He is the most ambitious man I have ever encountered, and if you recall Madame David's words regarding his pro-spects you will remember that she said he would be of little importance when we married, but would then attain great re-

nown and rule the world. You would easily imagine him thusly should you ever encounter him. I am happy beyond belief, and of course, Eugène idolizes him and may be able to serve in his command, which would ease my constant worry for his safety. General Buonoparte was exactly Eugène's age, fourteen, when he received his first commission in the army. We will marry in March and remain in Paris. How I wish you could be here.

Hortense is already a young lady of twelve and reminds me little of myself at that age, as she is cultured, well behaved and a gifted composer of music. As mother of a daughter I now shudder at the memory of my terrible behavior, and feel grateful she does not resemble me in that regard.

Please write me of your news and by the time this reaches you, the marriage banns will already have been published. If only you could be here with me to celebrate my happiness.

I close, as ever your devoted cousin,
Rose

February 7, 1796

Dearest cousin Rose,

How overjoyed I am for you and your forthcoming marriage. I too wish I could be there, but of course I am unable to leave my beloved Empire. Since the death of my dear friend, Mihrisah, the Sultan's mother, I now occupy the position of Valide Sultana, Mother of the Heir. As such, I am responsible for the welfare of the Empire's women and children, our schools, hospitals, public baths and other public buildings. It is an enormous task that requires more attention than I have ev-

er paid or needed to pay to anything. My life is quite exciting in ways I never imagined it might be.

Mahmud has become quite the young gentleman, an excellent swordsman as well as poet. He straddles what I have come to think of as our two cultures, despite the fact that he has never set foot on French soil.

Your new government continues to help us in our efforts towards modernization and our newly trained soldiers all speak French. I wonder if you or your betrothed may perhaps know General Aubert du Bayet, who is acting as our unofficial French Ambassador? Surely your friend Monsieur Barras knows him. He recently arrived to instruct our troops and help us build foundries for cannon. In return, Sultan Selim plans to appoint the first Turkish ambassador to France. So, you see, despite the distance between us, our two countries have begun to act as we do — as loving cousins.

Who could have imagined our lives as they are, and did you ever believe so many of the old obeah woman's predictions would actually come true? Perhaps your forthcoming marriage will truly fulfill your fate, and we will both be "queens" after all. Each year, it becomes more difficult to recall how young and carefree we once were on that little island.

I wish you much happiness in your coming marriage, and will always remain your loving cousin,
Aimée

Rose found it ironic to receive Aimée's letter on the first day of spring, which they had celebrated together as girls on Martinique. She read the letter and wished her new husband was there to share her excitement. Now she would need to write him about Aimée's astonishing news, when she would have preferred to read it to him instead. He had left for the Austrian front on the eleventh of March, just two days after they exchanged wedding vows, and she had already received seven letters. She wondered how he had time to fight, with all that writing, but loved his romantic verbal lovemaking too much to tease him. Paul Barras had been correct—the young man was certainly passionate. Unfortunately, he was also absent, and Rose preferred constant companionship and social stimulation. When they met, she was already the toast of Parisian salons, and now that she was married to a hero of the Revolution, thrived on the complimentary attention. Recently, it seemed she communicated with those she cared for most by letters: Eugène, Aimée, Hortense and Napoleon, as he was now known. When she finished reading Aimée's letter, she retrieved the first letter Napoleon had written her from an ornate olive wood box on her writing table. It was a proclamation of his passionate love, following their first assignation.

February 24, 1796
Seven o'clock in the morning.

My darling Josephine,
My waking thoughts are all of thee. Your portrait and the remembrance of last night's delirium have robbed my senses of repose. Sweet and incomparable Josephine, what an extraordinary influence you have over my heart. Are you vexed? Do I see you sad? Are you ill at ease? My soul is broken with grief,

and there is no rest for your lover. But is there more for me when, delivering ourselves up to the deep feelings which master me, I breathe out upon your lips, upon your heart, a flame which burns me up; ah, it was this past night I realized that your portrait was not you. You start at noon; I shall see you in three hours. Meanwhile, mi dolce amore, accept a thousand kisses, but give me none, for they fire my blood.
N. B.

She grinned broadly and pressed the paper to her heart. I love that he calls me Josephine. What an extraordinary young man. To think I initially thought him a curious little imp. *Quelle surprise!* She remembered the first time he called her Josephine. Following the announcement of their engagement, they were being feted at her friend Thèrèsa Tallein's, seated side by side at the table. One of her close friends addressed her from across the table, and when the exchange was over, he turned to her and asked, "I do not believe you have ever spoken your full given name to me, Madame. Will you please?"

She replied slowly with a slight smile, "Marie-Josèphe Rose de Tascher de la Pagerie de Beauharnais," she replied.

He thought for a moment, then said, "Marie and Josèphe are far too ordinary for you, which is no doubt why everyone calls you Rose. But, I think a more appropriate and feminine version of your name is Josephine."

"Josephine?"

"Yes, it flows more beautifully. Josephine de Beauharnais, or should I say Josephine Buonoparte? Either way, it is more mellifluous than Rose, do you not agree?"

"Josephine Buonoparte," she said, trying it out. "Yes, I believe you are correct, Monsieur."

"Now, try saying it a little differently: Josephine Bonaparte."

"Bonaparte?" she asked. "Are you changing your name as well as mine?"

"Only the spelling, just the deletion of two letters. But it brings out the French provenance. Don't you agree?"

She laughed and said, "I do agree, Monsieur."

He stood and raised his glass of champagne to everyone at the table, who raised theirs in turn, saying, "To long life and infinite happiness for Josephine and Napoleon Bonaparte!"

The next day, she wrote to tell Aimée about her new name. In a rare moment of reflection she thought it interesting that both she and her cousin were beginning the second half of their lives with new names.

Chapter 14

During the first nine years of Selim's reign, he slowly modified many of the old traditions of protocol and dress that he viewed as cumbersome and antiquated. He replaced elaborate formal headdresses of turbans or conical hats with the simpler fez. The meticulously proscribed combinations of pantaloons, robes, vests and belts disappeared in favor of simple tunics and leggings. The formal royal reception room in the Divan, where previously visitors had been carried before the Sultan, was now only used for occasions of state. Several new informal rooms within the palace were regularly used for meetings with military and political advisors. All of these changes began moving the Empire towards the modernity he expected the new century to bring. They also helped to increase Selim's availability to those who ran the government and his participation in governance.

The messenger, who now stood before the Sultan in one of these informal rooms, had crossed the Mediterranean from Cairo to Ephesus, roughly five hundred and twenty nautical miles, in a little more than five days, and then ridden over land another three hundred miles to Istanbul. Growing unrest in the Southern portions of the Empire—Syria and Egypt—had inspired the new relay system that utilized Baba's fastest ships for crossing the Mediterranean and men on horseback riding between stations exchanging tired mounts for fresh ones. Replacements at the stations relieved exhausted riders, and the peerless Arabian horses enabled riders to travel up to seventy-five miles a day on land, while with good wind a ship could travel more than one hundred nautical miles in a twenty-four hour period. The entire trip had taken only ten days to complete—half the time of the overland route.

Selim unfurled the carefully rolled document and read:

2 July, 1798

Bonaparte, member of the National Institute, General-in-Chief To the good people of Egypt,

For a long time, the Beys governing Egypt have insulted the French nation and its traders. The hour of their punishment has come. For too long this assortment of slaves bought in Georgia and the Caucasus has tyrannized the most beautiful part of the world; but God, on Whom all depends, has ordained that their empire is finished.

Peoples of Egypt, you will be told that I have come to destroy your religion; do not believe it! Reply that I have come to restore your rights, to punish the usurpers, and that I respect more than the Mamlūk God, His Prophet, and the Quran. Tell them that all men are equal before God; that wisdom, talents, and virtue alone make them different from one another. But, what wisdom, what talents, what virtues distinguish the Mamlūks that they should possess exclusively that which makes life pleasant and sweet?

Is there a good piece of farmland? It belongs to the Mamlūks. Is there...a fine horse, a beautiful house? They belong to the Mamlūks.

If Egypt is their farm, let them show the lease which God has granted them. But God is just and merciful to the people. All Egyptians will be called to administer all places; the best educated, the wisest and the most virtuous will govern, and the people will be happy.

Of old, there used to exist here, in your midst, big cities, big canals, and a thriving commerce. What has destroyed all this, but Mamlūk's greed, injustice, and tyranny?

Religious and military leaders, tell the people that we are the friends of the true Muslims.

Did we not destroy the Pope, who said that war should be waged against the Muslims? Did we not destroy the Knights of Malta because those insane people thought that God wanted them to wage war against the Muslims? Have we not been for centuries the friends of the Ottoman Sultan (may God fulfill his wishes!) and the engines of his engines? Have not the Mamlūks, on the contrary, always revolted against the authority of the Sultan, whom they still ignore? They do nothing but satisfy their own whims.

Thrice happy are those who join us! They shall prosper in wealth and rank. Happy are those who remain neutral! They will have time to know us and they will take our side. But unhappiness, threefold unhappiness to those who are themselves for the Mamlūks and fight against us! There shall be no hope for them; they shall perish.

Article 1. All villages within a radius of three leagues from the locations through which the army will pass will send a deputation to inform the Commanding General that they are obedient, and to notify him that they have hoisted the army flag: blue, white and red.

Article 2. All villages taking up arms against the French army shall be burnt down.

Article 3. All villages submitting to the army will hoist, together with the Ottoman flag, that of the army.

Article 4. The religious leaders shall have seals placed on the possessions, houses and properties belonging to the Mam-lūks, and will see that nothing is looted.

Article 5. The religious leaders shall continue to perform their functions. Each inhabitant shall remain at home, and prayers shall continue as usual. Each man shall thank God for the destruction of the Mamlūks and shall shout "Glory to the Ottoman Sultan! Glory to the French Army, friend!" May the Mamlūks be cursed, and the peoples of Egypt blessed!

Bonaparte

The Sultan was stunned to see his name affixed to a proclamation of which he had no prior knowledge. His messengers had been delivering regular communications since the French ships landed in Egypt two months earlier. But their presence appeared to be nothing more than part of the continual war between the French and the British. While the British controlled Cairo, they blocked French trade. But, the proclamation targeted the

Mamlūks, warrior slaves who governed both Egypt and Syria for two hundred years with the Sultan's reserved consent. They did so beneath his banner, and no one disputed the fact these were territories of the Ottoman Empire.

The *Mamlūks* had overthrown and defeated kings to become Egyptian sultans, and ruled within the careful scrutiny of the empire. They would fight fiercely to defend their territory, but would be no match for the modern, more sophisticated weaponry of the French. The *Mamlūks* losing battles to the French leant great support to the purpose of Selim's new Turkish army. Perhaps it might be an opportunity to rid Egypt of the slave leaders who were just as unstable as the Janissaries, whose allegiance shifted like the wind. That they had overthrown rulers to seize power in the first place was an unsettling fact he'd had to live with.

Koca Usef Pasha, now a general in the new army, stood beside the messenger and waited for the Sultan to finish reading the document before speaking.

"The French have captured Alexandria," he said. "Fortunately, Ben Osman's captains know all of the secret, hidden bays, or we would not be here. Napoleon's army marches south, towards Cairo. I have taken the liberty to assemble my men and alert the captains of the riflemen of the Corps of Gardeners. General Napoleon cannot turn back now, my lord, I believe he intends to take Egypt."

"And what else, I wonder?" Selim mused. Egypt provided access for Turkish trade routes to Europe, and Europe's access to Africa and Asia.

The Sultan addressed the Grand Vizier, who stood at attention on the opposite side of the room. "Summon General Aubert du Bayet to a private audience with me tomorrow morning immediately following morning prayers. Install the Valide Sultana behind the screen to translate should there be a need. Also summon the British Ambassador, Mr. Smith, for a later appointment. Make sure the two gentlemen pass each other as they depart and arrive. Arrange for all of my military advisors and generals to assemble in the Hall of the Divan immediately following the second meeting. This Napoleon is an ambitious man."

When he was alone, Selim read the proclamation again and thought the young general seemed to be just as brash as Rose had suggested. He wondered what other information Nakshidil might be able to discover from her cousin. He did not relish the idea of another war, as he was already fighting the Russians. A new war would complicate the issues with the Janissaries as well, and whose side would his French officers choose should he go to war with France? This was a particularly complicated political and military quandary, and the world was rife with revolutions—the Americas, France, Spain and Portugal, as well as some of his own territories. And why should the Janissaries be different from the Mamlūks? Both were armies of former slaves, and what do slaves always desire? Freedom and revenge. What might ever prepare a slave to rule? Nothing.

July 14, 1798

Dearest cousin Josephine,

It is my fervent hope that you and your children are well, and that the news I hear of the new French government is indeed true—that the five-man Directory is governing fairly, and the French people are no longer hungry or disquieted. But imagine my shocked surprise to learn that your husband, General Bonaparte, has invaded our sovereign territory of Egypt and claims he did so on the Sultan's behalf! I read his proclamation to the Egyptian people, in which he clearly states this. I am confused as to why you made no mention of such a plan to me. Is it possible you did not know of your husband's intent to travel to our Empire?

The severity of the situation forces me to be forthright and beg you to enlighten us to his intentions. If in truth he desires to ally himself to us, why act in secrecy? We can think of no reason other than a wish to surprise and conquer. Please tell me this is not so, for if it is, then we are at war with our beloved France.

I am sending this to you in much haste, before meeting with your ambassador, Monsieur Aubert du Bayet, tomorrow. Please respond in equal haste. The thought of our sons and loved ones facing each other in battle is more than I can bear. Please respond quickly!

I am Nakshidil, Valide Sultana of the Ottoman Empire, but please remember that I am yet and shall always remain your loving cousin,

Aimée

On the next day, immediately following his meetings with the ambassadors and his advisors, Selim ordered the formation of an additional Turkish Regiment to be *hired* rather than conscripted. It would be the first Turkish army of free men in over five hundred years. The recruits would be brought from Anatolia, a province of Turkey, and be trained at Uskudar, outside the city. The new troops would add twenty thousand men to Selim's secret army.

Couriers arrived steadily for the next few weeks to report Napoleon's movements, while Selim's new army trained at a furious pace to ready themselves for battle.

~ ~ ~

In the Egyptian desert, General Napoleon Bonaparte, an avid student of history, Greek philosophy and ancient wars, dismounted and dropped to his knees when, from a distance of three kilometers, he first glimpsed the Great Pyramid. He had never felt more excited in his life.

"We are looking at the very same wondrous structure seen by Alexander the Great three hundred years before the birth of Christ Jesus." he said to the man at his side, Chief Engineer Jacques-Marie Le Pére.

"I could not discern his presence in Alexandria," Napoleon continued, "the city he designed and built. It has been overrun by foreigners far too long. Did you know that the main thoroughfare of the city is oriented toward the rising sun on Alexander's birthday?" he asked.

"I did not know that," Le Pére replied.

"Of course, our engagement with the *Mamlūks* in Alexandria was also a huge distraction. But this pyramid seems untouched by humanity or time. It stands as it always has, unencumbered by man's folly, unconcerned by the passage of time. What an honor it is to stand before it."

The entire retinue of eight hundred men had come to a stop, and now stood gawking at the extraordinary sight. Most were not students of history like their general. The soldiers who knew what the pyramid was began explaining the structure to others, causing an excited exchange among the men.

"Monsieur La Pére, have you ever seen a structure of this size?" Napoleon asked.

"No, my general. I doubt that any Frenchman has."

Napoleon stood in awe and wonder imagining how such a gargantuan edifice might have been engineered and the manpower it had taken to build it. "Let's have a closer look, and make camp in its shadow," Napoleon said, mounting his horse and galloping forward.

When they reached the base of the Great Pyramid, Napoleon dismounted and gave orders to assemble his troops. After the men had lined up in formation, he stood on an improvised platform and addressed them.

"You stand at attention because we are the first Frenchmen to rest in the shadow of the Great Pyramid, built more than four-thousand years ago by a Pharaoh of Egypt. Two-thousand years later, Alexander the Great, ruler of the world

*and architect of Alexandria, stood where we now stand and
founded a new dynasty, the Ptolemaic Dynasty, which ruled
Egypt for three hundred years! Perhaps some of you know the
story of Cleopatra, who brought an end to that dynasty by her
doomed alliance with the Roman Mark Antony. I wish you to
know these things so that you might offer proper reverence to
this place and to know that each and every one of you shall
also be a part of history now. I have no doubt the Mamlūks
will find us here and attempt to dissuade us from our task, but
we must not allow them to do so. Soldiers, forty centuries are
watching you."*

~ ~ ~

On the thirtieth of July, Sultan Selim received dis-
quieting news. Napoleon's forces had prevailed once
more against the *Mamlūks* at Gizeh and the pyramids
were now in the possession of the French. On the following day, Napoleon marched unimpeded into Cairo
where he met no resistance from the Egyptian people.
But rather than looting and killing, to everyone's surprise, the general sent word to dozens of the ruling
Sheiks inviting them to meet with him. Believing it to be
a trap, the Sheiks initially refused. A few days later, they
had a change of heart and capitulated to his request.
Once in his presence, the Sheiks were surprised to learn
that he did not wish to conquer or rule. He wanted to
"set them free." He had even laid out and offered to
them a plan for their new independence. They were to
choose a ruling Divan of fourteen leaders from within

their tribes to govern themselves. No invading army had ever made such a request.

~ ~ ~

During the time the Sheiks were organizing them-selves into a new government, Napoleon's cadre of engineers, cartographers, Masons, scientists and artists measured, recorded, mapped and illustrated the pyramids and the visible head and neck of the sphinx. No European had ever before seen structures such as these. Their awe and excitement were palpable. How amazed their countrymen would be when they brought the renderings and proof of their findings home. They had no doubt that their General Napoleon would join the ranks of Alexander the Great and Marco Polo.

~ ~ ~

On September the first, 1798, Aimée received the answer to her letter—unfortunately, too late to prevent Selim from declaring war on France.

Dearest, dearest cousin,

Please be comforted and relieved when I tell you that my husband has no intention of conquering your Empire! I assure you, that is not his intention. When last I saw him, at Christmas, we discussed his forthcoming trip to Egypt, and it was with great trepidation he embarked upon that journey. He did so only at the insistence of The Directory. It is my husband's belief that they wish him to fail in this endeavor, secretly hoping for his defeat either at the hands of the British or the Egyptians. That is an empty desire, I assure you, as my husband will not court defeat. One would think The Directory would wish him to succeed in any effort, but they have become jealous of anyone who garners consistent success, and my husband's successes have already become heroic. Mind you, I do not pretend to understand these matters fully, as I have no expertise in the intricacies of such politics.

As to why Bonaparte did not first inform the Sultan of his intentions regarding Egypt, I cannot say. But please, have faith in my word and his, for he is, above all, an honorable man. Fear not his presence, for there is a greater purpose for his trip. I tell you this in the strictest confidence, as he has not shared it with The Directory. As a result of my husband's ceaseless survey of a wide array of knowledge, he believes there exists, in Egypt, an ancient canal linking the Mediterranean with the Red Sea. This may be his most ambitious and far-fetched notion yet, if such a canal indeed exists, it would shorten the trip from France by thousands of nautical miles, turning a treacherous journey around the Cape of Good Hope that usually takes more than two months into a mere three or four weeks! If we are able to locate and rebuild the canal, we not only gain shortened trade routes, we may simultaneously block the British access to their most prosperous colonial holding, India. Even I understand the possible benefit of this. Imagine being able to transport silk and spices from the East in a matter of weeks! I pray his notion prevails and for his safety in this adventure. I have not had word from him since he embarked from Toulon in May, as he was unable to spare a ship for the transportation of correspondence. I find myself missing his letters, which usually arrive daily, even during wartime.

In light of The Directory's perceived intentions, Bonaparte keeps Eugène by his side as aide-de-camp, where he will not engage in battle. I pray daily for their safe return. Hortense is here in Paris with me, and the belle of Paris! I know not which one of us adores this city more, and am happy to say that it is, once again, the most exciting of places. I am always entertained, rarely without company and never bored despite my husband's long absences.

Please continue to keep me informed of the events in your life, as I will keep you apprised of mine.

I remain and always shall remain,
Your devoted cousin,
Rose

Nakshidil immediately brought the letter to Selim and sat opposite him until he had finished reading. She knelt at his feet, her hands grasping his. She looked up at him and pleaded.

"He does not mean to conquer us," she said. "Why must we make war on our ally, the country of my ancestors, the country that has been so generous to us? French officers trained our army, built our foundries and filled our armories with guns and cannon." Tears streamed down her face.

"You may be the only person more sorry than I about this war, but I cannot allow anyone to govern my empire without my blessing, without my guidance and certainly not without my agreement. I know you understand that well, Naksh, and if it were any country other than France, you would not be asking me these questions."

She wiped the tears from her cheeks. "Of course, you are correct, but I cannot help think there has been a great misunderstanding somewhere in this. And I do believe Rose."

"You may very well be correct in that, but I must act upon the actual facts of the matter and not supposition. General Napoleon has invaded our sovereign territory of Egypt, defeated the *Mamlūks* in several battles, taken possession of Cairo and is building a fortress less than twenty miles from Alexandria. He has not communicated with me in any other way, and I must assume that he means to disempower me. And why should he stop at Egypt's borders? Why not take Syria as well?"

"My mind knows you are right, but my heart refuses to follow," she said.

"Believe me, I understand. But he must be stopped, and I can only hope our troops are up to the task. I recently met with the brother of the English ambassador, Sidney Smith, an admiral in the British navy. He is here visiting his brother after a partial retirement, whatever that may be, and has suggested an alliance with us."

"An alliance with the English?" she asked incredulously.

"Yes, the English. It is said that war makes strange bedfellows, Naksh."

Chapter 15

Nakshidil reclined on an ornate divan beneath a gold cupola in the magnificent private garden that had formerly belonged to the Circassian Kadine. Three years had passed since her friend's untimely death, and she was finally beginning to feel comfortable in the older woman's apartments as well as her position. One of her hands rested in her lap, cradling the pile of diamonds that gathered there from the long strand that wound around her neck—the only priceless rope that remained after the murder of her friend. Selim had wanted her to have it, and now she worked the stones like a rosary, silently repeating the prayer to the Blessed Virgin. She did not remember when reciting the rosary had become a part of her life again, but it brought her great comfort in difficult times, of which there seemed to be many of late.

The war with France in Egypt had been disruptive, despite the ultimate Ottoman victory. It appeared that General Bonaparte truly cared more for his excavations and explorations than for conquering. After losing critical battles at Abū Qīr Bay, Rosetta and Acre to the combined English and Turkish forces, Napoleon secretly fled Egypt and sailed home to France.

In fact, it was France itself he truly wished to conquer and rule—and that is exactly what he did. Rose had written to say that upon his return in early November, her husband had dissolved The Directory as well as the Council of Five Hundred in an unopposed *coup d'état* that took only three days. Then, less than a month later, on Christmas Eve, he announced the formation of a new Consulate of the French Republic, a three-man legislature headed by himself as First Consul. Selim pronounced the move as "brilliant—a peaceful coup that will put an end to the Revolution once and for all and, unlike the former kings, Napoleon is a hero and man of the people."

"It seems that everyone in France supports him," Nakshidil said after carefully reading every article in every French newspaper they had received in their last shipment. "Did you know that he brought the wonders of Egypt for all of France to see?" she asked Selim. "The Louvre has already begun to exhibit the treasures. They include," she said reading from one paper, "'precious papyrus scrolls, statuary, a variety of items of blown glass, gold and copper jewelry, preserved human mummies in burial cases and a mysterious stone of unknown origin—a large block of black basalt, precisely carved with unintelligible ancient inscriptions—excised from an ancient stone wall near the town of Rosetta, twenty kilometers east of Abū Qīr Bay.' How extraordinary! I wish I could see them."

"I wish I could have made him pay for them," Selim

responded. "He puts his plunder on display and they say that we are the barbarians."

"I had not thought of it in that way," she said quietly.

"Of course not my love, because in your heart, you still think like a French woman."

She instantly realized he was right. "And do you not still enjoy that sometimes?" She teased.

"As often as you care to share it, my Aimée," he responded.

"In that case, I command you to reveal yourself to me now," she said unfastening the ties of her gown to expose her breasts. "Hold yourself for me," she said with a smile, sliding her silk pantaloons off and spreading her legs wide. In three years, they still had not tired of this game. She held her nether lips open for him to see as he strained to release his hardening penis from his pants. "Make it very hard," she said, "so I can ride it."

Afterwards, when they were both beginning to breathe normally again he said, "I never would have guessed you'd become aroused by reading a list of artifacts."

~ ~ ~

When Selim received news that Napoleon's book, *Description de l'Égypte* had been published, he asked Pierre Ruffin to secure a copy for him. The volume contained the first of eight hundred engravings rendered by the artists who accompanied Napoleon on his Egyptian mission. The remainder of the engravings would ultimately fill twenty-two more volumes.

By early February, following Napoleon's ascension to power, the books became so popular that printings barely kept pace with the demand of sales. All things Egyptian began to permeate Parisian society, from furniture to fashion, makeup and hairstyles, jewelry and art.

Napoleon's men had personally transported the artifacts to France. And the enthusiastic reception of the astounding items completely overshadowed the military defeat, which went virtually unnoticed. He and his expedition were heralded like returning heroes for being the first Europeans to witness and record the wonders of the ancient world. Napoleon had found more archaeological treasure than he ever dreamed possible: the pyramids, the sphinx, the tombs and temples of Philae, Dendera, Luxor and the Valley of the Kings. Now all of it was on exhibit at the Louvre.

~ ~ ~

When Aimée asked Rose if the canal he sought had been found, she replied that he had indeed *"found incontrovertible proof of the ancient canal linking the Mediterranean to the Red Sea. The attending experts agreed that the remains of the canal's construction were over one thousand years old and, very possibly, many times older, as it appeared to have been previously reconstructed. Unfortunately, his chief engineer, Monsieur Jacques-Marie Le Pére, estimated the Red Sea to be thirty feet higher than the Mediterranean. This difference in height would necessitate building an impossibly costly system of locks entailing ten or more years of construction. But it was exciting and gratifying to learn that the canal did exist as he believed."*

~ ~ ~

As the new century began in Paris, Napoleon's exploits were all anyone cared to discuss, and his wife, Josephine, became first lady of the New French Republic. After signing the treaty of Amiens, which provided a brief respite from the ongoing war between France and Great Britain, Napoleon focused on rebuilding his beloved country. It was during this time of relative peace that he quietly returned the Egyptian territories he had been occupying. This allowed Selim to refocus his attention at home and continue to build his new army. Nine thousand troops, highly trained in Western warfare, openly moved into barracks overlooking the Golden Horn. Selim's new army had become a reality. The Janissaries continued to refuse to recognize or train with the new "infidel" soldiers, and the seeds of revolution spread in earnest throughout the Empire. Fundamentalist factions from as far away as Egypt and Syria began to unite against Sultan Selim III, and no one understood the portent of that union better than he. It would not take long before the rebellious forces joined with the Janissaries and he feared that together they would have the power to overthrow the throne.

~ ~ ~

The war between their empires had left a gap in Rose and Aimée's correspondence and after more than a year, a letter finally arrived from France.

February 26, 1802

> *My dearest, dearest,*
> *Can you ever forgive my long silence? I only hope you may as no one more than you will understand the import of my current life. I am Consort of the Republic of France, wife of the First Consul, ruler of France! Who but you, dear cousin, might ever have believed that all of Madame David's words would indeed come to pass? It may have been forethought on her part to not warn us of the war between our two empires, yet, it passed without either of our houses suffering personal loss, and seems not to have left any scars here in France, as I hope is also true with you. Please tell me this is so.*
> *I have had the great fortune to see with my own eyes the magnificent renditions of many amazing wonders of your land which appears to be as you have always indicated, more so-phisticated than our own. I now understand more fully your devotion to your new home. How happy you must truly be to live amongst such art and beauty.*
> *How is your son, Mahmud? Eugène returned to Paris almost three years ago after suffering a minor wound, and is now a Brigadier General in the Army of Italy. I am sorry to say that he rarely visits Paris. Hortense recently married my brother in law, Louis-Napoleon, who I pray will make a good match despite the discrepancy in years between them. He is*

old enough to be her father but has excellent prospects, as you may imagine, and Hortense is already with child. I am to be a grand-mère!

I am most excited to tell you that Bonaparte has appointed an old friend from Corsica, Baron Horace François Bastien Sébastiani, as our first official ambassador to the Ottoman Empire. He will arrive soon with his wife, Fanny, a personal friend of mine whom I know you will enjoy meeting. I have sent a small gift for you with her and hope you will receive them both with pleasure.

I pray you forgive my long silence and my husband's transgressions and that we may continue our correspondence once again. Despite distance and war and empires, I shall always remain your loving and devoted cousin,

Rose / Josephine

Aimée closed her eyes and sighed deeply. *Oh, Rose,* she thought, *of course I'll always love you.* When she opened her eyes, her son stood before her and she was no longer the young girl on Martinique.

"Mother, have you acted upon my wishes?" he asked.

She had been caught off guard by Mahmud's request, had almost laughed aloud in response and was unable to answer immediately.

"Mother?" Mahmud said without hiding his annoyance. "I come to you in respect of your position as Valide Sultana. It is only fitting that you should bring a choice of appropriate women before me. I am nineteen years old, after all."

She smiled broadly. Would she always think of him

as her little boy? "Of course, Mahmud. You are quite correct. It is certainly time. Please forgive me for not making the suggestion sooner myself. You have spoken of this with your uncle?"

"Yes. It was he that suggested I make the request directly to you, as was proper."

She could not stifle her grin, and bowed her head to cough artificially into her hand, stalling for a moment to control herself. "Of course," she said again. "Allow me a few days to think about this properly and to query my ladies. I promise we shall find you several appropriate...(she almost said 'girls') young women."

"They need not be too young, Mother," he said. "And I would prefer a woman who is not a virgin, if you think that appropriate, of course. Uncle has suggested that a young woman with some experience might be preferable."

"By all means, Mahmud. I shall do my best and make arrangements as quickly as possible. Have you any other preferences I might consider?"

He thought for a moment and answered in a serious tone. "I would like her to be pleasing to look upon and perhaps a graceful dancer."

"Good for you. A comely dancer is always a pleasure to behold. I promise to bear all your requests in mind when making my choices." *And mine as well*, she thought. *She must be intelligent and clever, worthy of holding counsel for a ruler of empires.*

After he left, she didn't know whether to laugh or cry. Her little boy was already a young man, and that meant she was no longer a young woman. But she still felt like one. How was that possible at thirty-nine years? She mostly sensed the passage of time in events that faded a little more each year: her childhood, the years in the convent, her sojourn in Paris, Mr. Braugham, her abduction, the old Sultan and dear, dear Baba, the only ghost from her past who was still in her life.

In fact, the recent discontent fomented by the Janissaries had once again necessitated the arrival of Baba's fleet to their harbor. A new sinister plot seemed to be brewing. During the previous week, the Kizlar Agasi reported hundreds of cartoon drawings scrawled on walls throughout the city. The crude pictures depicted the Sultan as a eunuch. Simultaneously, fundamentalist factions within the Divan had circulated rumors of Selim's impotency. The combination of the two caused quite an uproar and the first open opposition to Selim. Everyone in the palace feared the Janissaries might revolt and if they did, they would outnumber Selim's army by ten thousand men or more.

All the palace guards were on alert, even Cavus Hamza, who clung to the shadows like a spider waiting for the right moment to pounce.

Chapter 16

March 1805

Fannie Bastien, the French Ambassador's wife who now regularly visited Nakshidil, sat quietly in an Empire-style chair, her arms resting on the carved and gilded wings of a swan. Upholstered in peach-colored jacquard silk, the chair had recently arrived from Paris along with several others. It was a flawless example of the Egyptian designs that flooded the markets of Paris in recent years. The young woman always welcomed the moments she was not engaged in conversation with the Sultana, as it gave her freedom to observe details of the magnificent apartments. The low oval table on which trays of coffee were served was her favorite—a solid slab of precious lapis lazuli polished so highly one could almost see one's reflection in the surface. In France, the stone was so rare it was only seen in tiny pea-sized bits set into rings or ear bobs. At the moment, the table reflected a soft, amber glow from elegantly sculpted alabaster oil sconces that graced the walls. The walls themselves were extraordinary, made of intricately carved fragrant cedar wood. One wall had two tall windows framing French doors leading to the private garden.

Priceless works of art, beautiful enough to rival the treasures Napoleon had brought back from Egypt, occupied every surface. Following each of her visits, the Ambassador's wife meticulously recorded not only the details of their conversations, but also descriptions and illustrations of clothing, jewelry, furniture, objects d'art and food. The pages of one small leather-bound journal had already been filled.

When Nakshidil finished reading the letter Fannie had brought, an expression of incredulity spread across her face. She rested the letter in her lap and whispered to herself, "Empress of France? *Mon dieu*, it is true."

"Yes, Your Grace, quite true, I assure you," Fannie replied.

"No, no," Nakshidil laughed. "I did not doubt the veracity. I meant...something else. It is of no importance," she said dismissively. "*Mon dieu*," she repeated, "Rose is Napoleon's Empress." Her mind immediately began replaying the scene of the two young girls sitting on the earthen floor of the old *obeah* woman's hut. "Two queens!" they had shrieked. "Two queens," she said aloud.

"To be sure, Your Grace, a Sultana and an Empress," Fanny said. "Two cousins and two queens."

"You must forgive me, Madame," Nakshidil said, shaking her head and laughing softly. "I was thinking of another time and place." She signaled a serving girl who waited quietly in the far corner of the room. Within moments, the girl entered carrying a tray with coffee service and an ebony bowl of gold-dipped almonds that she placed on the lapis table.

"Would you like some fruits or sweets?" Nakshidil asked, "or perhaps a glass of champagne? Yes! That is exactly what this occasion calls for." She barely raised one finger to the serving girl, who immediately left.

"Oh, I would dearly love to see her," Nakshidil mused.

"Would a journey to France not be possible, your grace?"

"Quite possible, Madame, but I would not choose to make such a trip. At my age, I have too many comforts that could not be met, and I am needed here now more than ever. But let's not discuss such things at a moment like this. Let us rather celebrate the very good fortune of my dearest cousin."

The servant reappeared with a gold tray bearing an open bottle of French champagne and two crystal glasses that she rested on an ornately carved sideboard. She expertly poured two glasses, handed one to each woman, and then retired into the shadows.

Nakshidil raised her glass aloft. "To the Empress Josephine Bonaparte. May she be blessed with health and happiness."

The women drank their toast. Then Fannie added, "and bear many sons."

Nakshidil paused a moment with her glass raised before drinking. She carefully read the expression on her friend's face and saw no sarcasm in it. Perhaps she did not know Rose's age. Frenchwomen were very secretive about such things, and Fannie could not have been more than twenty-five years herself. *Might Rose bear another child? If she were able, why had she not in the last eight years of her marriage? They were both mature women of forty-one now.*

"Yes, God willing," Nakshidil added with a smile. *Whatever god may pay attention to such things,* she thought.

Later that day, she wrote a letter to Rose.

March 1, 1805

> *My dearest, darling cousin,*
>
> *I am thrilled to learn of your extreme good fortune, and bow deeply to the new Empress of France. How I wish I were there to see for myself, but perhaps it is best I am not, as I remember well my appalling lack of success amongst Parisian society. Mon dieu, I am happy to be able to laugh at that terrible episode now—my failure was surely kismet. But you, my dear, you are an Empress!*
>
> *Thank you so much for sending Madame Sébastiani to me. You cannot imagine how wonderful it is to speak French with a Frenchwoman after more than twenty years. I did not realize how much I had missed it and how good it makes me feel. She is delightful and visits often. Today, after reading your wonderful news, we drank a toast to your good health and fortune.*
>
> *Your happy news and all the talk of France made me quite melancholy, an emotion I rarely allow myself to indulge as it only brings unhappiness. Did not Madame David mention something to this effect, that we would miss our carefree lives on Martinique? I remember those years so vaguely now that it makes me feel quite old. But today I realized how fully I embrace my life here and how I have come to feel at home here*

also—so much that I choose not to leave, even for a visit to see you.

Mahmud and Sultan Selim are both quite well despite the current unrest in our territories that has begun to spread its poison to our shores. It is not the first time we have faced such adversity, but seems to me more violent than in the past. I fear we may also face a revolution and I take some comfort in how well the French have survived theirs—although not without paying a price. There is an old saying in which I find solace— all things change. And so it is with this life, my dear Yeyette.

Yet, I remain as ever, your loving cousin,
Aimée

~ ~ ~

Two months later, Nakshidil would remember that day she had toasted the health of her cousin as the beginning of the end of a long period of contentment. "Josephine" was secure in her position as the most important woman in France, her eminence now mirrored Nakshidil's own, and the prophecy had been fulfilled. One of the things she still vividly recalled was how cavalier Rose had been about the final words of the prediction: "You will die miserable and alone." *We all die alone*, she thought. *Rose must have known that then.*

Now, the neatly woven fiber of Nakshidil's world felt as if it were beginning to unravel. A dark cloud hung over Selim and as he changed so had their relationship. She did not mind his other lovers, in fact it was her duty to encourage exactly that. As Valide Sultana, head of the harem, she brought appropriate women before him and helped him to choose. He currently had nine favorites and still shared his bed with her at least once a week. But the Valide Sultana was also the most politically powerful woman in the Empire. All of his other lovers had the luxury of distance from government problems, allowing them to focus solely on lovemaking. Frightening new developments had begun to encroach upon their untroubled happiness, and their weekly lovemaking had been replaced by long hours of discussions of problems, solutions and tactics. Selim was continually preoccupied and in actual fact, they had not made love for several months.

The political discord had begun with news from the Al-Hijaz region of Western Arabia, where a group of fundamentalist Islamic Muslims, popularly referred to as "Wahhabis," had done the unthinkable—attacked and desecrated the holy cities of Medina and Mecca. The sect, founded by a charismatic cleric named Muhammad Ibn Abd al-Wahhab, had been gathering momentum for almost sixty years. For centuries, Islam had casually morphed into two versions: strict Islamic Law as proscribed in the Quran, and "popular Islam" as practiced by the majority of Muslims. However, these distinctions were never acknowledged as separate until al-Wahhab began advocating his austere interpretation. He preached a vehement style of "pure Islam" that was radical enough to alienate many Muslims. The movement might have entered the oblivion of anonymity had he not joined forces with a local Emir, Muhammad Abd Ibn Saud. As head of the powerful Al Saud tribal family, he agreed to support "Wahhabism" in return for *bakshish*, small regular payments or tribute from each of al-Wahhab's followers.

The arrangement created the Arab Emirate of Diriyah (which would later become the first Saudi state), and revenues increased along with followers, giving the Al Saud family the power to challenge the Sultan. If they prevailed, they could become the sole independent rulers of Arabia. The Emirate, now under the leadership of the founder's sons, had an army of fifty thousand "true believers" dedicated to the purification of the Islamic faith. Their doctrine appealed to the greatest portion of the populace—the poor and uneducated—by condemning the comforts and luxuries that had become part of everyday life for many Muslims—opulent temples and homes, alcoholic spirits, jewelry, Western furniture, eating utensils, and styles of dress.

Wahhabism continued to grow, and now they had invaded Al-Hijaz, in Western Arabia. The area bordered the Red Sea and contained the two holiest cities in the Islamic world—Medina and Mecca. When they attacked and desecrated these, it brought the Wahhabi into conflict with the entire Islamic world and most notably, its Sultan.

As "Sovereign of the House of Osman, Sultan of Sultans, Commander of the Faithful and Protector of the Holy Cities of Mecca, Medina and Jerusalem, Emperor of the Three Cities of Constantinople, Adrianople and Bursa, and of the Cities of Damascus and Cairo, of All Azerbaijan, of the Magris, of Barka, of Kairuan, of Aleppo, of Arabic Iraq," etcetera, Selim was duty bound to act. All holy cities and sites were under his protection.

In the privacy of the Sultan's chambers, Nakshidil asked Selim, "What could they possibly hope to gain by the destruction of holy sites? Won't this turn the people against their cause?"

"The Wahhabis interpret the Quran in a very literal way, Naksh. And they see their interpretation as the *only* way. Who can ever say what someone's words meant when they were written, except the author himself?" He stood up and began pacing the room in an agitated state. "Scholars and priests have debated the words of the Quran forever. I believe that most Muslims follow the words of the Prophet as best they can, and who is truly able to say that someone else is doing it wrong?"

"I think that Christians do the same thing," Nakshidil said. "Different interpretations I mean. Catholics and Protestants certainly do not agree on the Bible's meaning and each is certain that they are right and the other is wrong."

"I find it infuriating!" Selim exclaimed. "These "true believers" are going too far. It is one thing to believe in your own truth but I cannot condone the imposition of that truth upon others who think differently. These Wahhabis are now stopping pilgrims along their routes to the holy shrines to force them to join their cause and to collect a tithe! They actually demand allegiance to their cause and *bakshish*, a fee to allow them to pass on to the holy cities."

"I have never heard of such a thing," she said.

"These pilgrims are traveling to Mecca to honor our dead prophets and the Wahhabis try to make this a sin. Why? How can they say that Allah does not want us to honor our dead, especially our dead prophets who were his teachers? This makes no sense and I cannot understand why anyone would find this reasonable."

"What exactly do the Wahabbi profess regarding this?" she asked.

"They maintain that luxury in any form is a sin against the teachings of the Quran. That renders all but the most rudimentary temples, sinful because they are beautiful and contain precious items related to worship. I do not believe the Quran forbids beauty or luxury for that matter. Even Christ Jesus who preached against the exchange of monies in the temples did not condemn beauty."

" And Christians worship images of Him and the Virgin Mother and the saints in all of their churches. Would these be considered luxuries?" she responded.

"Apparently, according to the Wahhabis." He sighed deeply and sat down again. "It might be better to ask why so many people fear change. Change appears to be the only thing one may reliably count on in this life, don't you agree? And yet, people fight to keep everything the same as it always was…as it always seemed to be, that is."

She laughed ruefully. "It does appear to be so."

"These people would see us remaining as we have been for four centuries. They would take us back to the Dark Ages if they could. At the heart, it is a rebellion against me and my desire to modernize an archaic political and social system. They are fools to believe they can stop progress. The world will not wait for us to catch up. It will destroy us—if they don't destroy us first."

"Will they come to Istanbul?"

"Not yet, but it is only a matter of time before they do, and *when* they do, the Janissaries will join them. Then what will we do?"

Nakshidil had no answer. The Janissaries had always been the proverbial thorn in their side, and if they joined forces with the Wahhabis, they would be too powerful to control. Their history of rebellion against the Sultanate was long and bloody, and there were now more of them than ever.

"How many men have we in the new army?" she asked.

"Not enough," he answered. "We have begun recruiting again in Anatolia, but it will take a year or more to hire and train enough men to fight them, and I don't know if we will be able to..." his voice trailed off.

"What about Baba Ben Osman's fleet and the loyal armies of the Pashas?"

"We will summon them all, Naksh. I loathe transforming our city into an armed camp, but we must prepare for war—a war against our own people, a revolution." He sighed deeply.

She walked to where he sat and stood directly in front of him. "Then allow me to distract you for a brief moment," she said, unfastening her outer robe and allowing it to slip to the floor. The only adornment on her naked body was the diamond belt she had worn on the night of her first assignation with the old Sultan. The six large stones hung from the clasp, between her nether lips.

"Naksh," he began to protest.

She lifted and held his chin in her right hand, stroking his hair with the other. "Listen to me, my love. You have many important things to occupy your mind, but you have forgotten the most important of all, your duty to please *me*."

"Naksh," he protested again.

"Sshhh," she said, placing a finger over his lips. "Aimée is here for you...only for you," she said, lowering herself onto his lap. She entwined her fingers in his hair, then gently tightened her grip. "Can you see how much I need you now?" She tilted her head back, unfastening her hair with one hand, gently shaking it, allowing it to cascade over her body. "Suckle my breast my love," she said, guiding his head towards her left nipple, as she unfastened the front of his trousers. "Bite me gently until you are hard, and then give me your cock."

"Aimée," he whispered as he entered her. It was the only word he uttered.

Later on, she regretted not having thought of it sooner. He had been wonderful. She was pleased that he still responded to her command, perhaps because she was the only woman able to command him. She smiled at the memory of recent pleasure and reminded herself to remember that she knew exactly how to awaken his need. *Wasn't life interesting and wonderful even when it was so uncertain?*

Chapter 17

While Selim prepared for revolution, *L'Empire fran-
çais* grew stronger and more powerful, as did Napoleon
himself. As the breadth of his realm increased, so did
Napoleon's need for heirs—sons who would carry his
seed of greatness. France adored their Emperor and
wanted his progeny to continue to rule the Empire in
perpetuity. The desire for such a legacy directly contra-
dicted Napoleon's love and adoration of his barren wife.
All of France knew that his mistress, Éléonore Denuelle,
had given birth to a son. The birth left no question of
impotence in the minds of the French citizenry, and they
demanded their Emperor fulfill his duty to sire legitimate sons.

May 7, 1807

> *Dearest cousin,*
> *How can life be so cruel to give and then take away our
> most treasured gifts? It pains me to tell you that my sweet
> first grandson, Napoleon Louis Charles, has passed from this
> life. He was a little angel at just five years old, leaving us and*

this life far too soon. Hortense mourns most painfully, and there is nothing to do or say to relieve her grief. The immediacy of her need now overshadows my own, and I have little desire to dwell upon the possible loss of another gift, my marriage and husband.

Six months ago, my husband's mistress, Madame Denuelle, gave birth to a baby boy. As you know, our marriage has been fruitless, and I believed the fault lay with him rather than me. The appearance of this bastard child has now revealed the terrible truth of my barrenness, and I cannot maintain my defense any longer.

Complicating matters further, the attributes I initially found so intoxicating in my husband's nature have now become a source of deep anxiety and grief. His love for power, possession and dominance appear to outweigh his love for me, and he feels the need to cast me aside unless I provide him with an heir. His formal adoption of Eugène might insure his place if only he had the constitution to fight for it. Sadly, it is not in my son's nature. My infertility has become the fodder for rumors that fly everywhere in Paris and now the public openly demands a royal heir. Mon dieu, chérie, I see no hope for our union, and I am devastated by the prospect of divorce. I do not believe myself strong enough to cope with more loss. I am simply not able.

Although I am Empress of France, I have few true friends in this world and only one, Mlle. Le Normand, in whom I may confide such terrible pain as this. I apologize if my grief and burden lie heavily on your gentle soul. It is proving difficult to recover from losses such as these.

Pray for me, dear cousin, if God still listens to your voice.
Rose

Rose did not mention the extraordinary turn of events that followed Napoleon's victories in wars against Austria, Prussia and Russia. She was too distracted by the prospect of divorce and unable to cope with anything other than her own personal loss. But Tsar Alexander had signed two peace treaties dividing almost the entirety of Europe between France and Russia. The treaties also established a blockade of British trade that allied all of Europe against Britain and included a hidden agenda—France and Russia joined forces against Turkey to take as much of the Ottoman Empire as possible. Now that Russia was an ally, Napoleon secretly began investigating the possibility of marriage within the Czar's family.

Unaware of the secret pact against him, Selim feared what the new allies might do if he lost control of the Sultanate. Would they swoop in and devastate his empire? If so, he would be attacked from without *and* within, as the Wahhabis continued gaining strength in both numbers and funds. As people were swept up in the pressure to choose sides, the gap between fundamentalist and secular Muslims grew wider. Many undecided citizens fell back on old prejudices, and the rift between Sunni and Shia grew steadily more violent. By the beginning of 1807, all territories of the Empire had clearly divided into two camps, moderate Suni or fundamentalist Shia. The first supported modernization and Sultan Selim, and the latter advocated a radical return to the past with a new sultan, Nuket Seza's son, Mustapha.

True to course, the Janissaries were in favor of the latter, gathering strength from the ongoing confrontations and increasing their numbers from fifty to one-hundred-thousand men. Backed by the Ulema of Islamic priests, the fundamentalists vowed to destroy all modern conveniences, luxuries, freedoms and European alliances—everything that had been so carefully put into place by Sultan Selim. However, the priests did not wish to be held responsible for the Sultan's murder, as the populace of Istanbul dearly loved him. The people would be more inclined to accept a new regime if Selim were alive, so the Ulema agreed to support the revolution only under those terms.

The new year began with an astounding occurrence. Abdullah Ibn Saud, leader of the Wahhabi crusade, ordered *his* name to replace the Sultan's in prayers in the great mosque. Worshipers were instructed to thank *Saud* for his beneficence, praise *Saud* for all they had been given and ask *Saud* to intercede on their behalf—instead of their sovereign. Calling himself the "purifier of the faith," he made it his holy mission to depose Selim. With the intention of besmirching The Sultan, Saud told his followers to embark on a campaign of rumors in Istanbul. They were to spread the word that the attacks on Mecca and Medina had been "divine retribution" for Selim's modernizations and "infidel innovations." The infidel Sultan must be overthrown lest all of Islam pay the price for his transgressions. Chaos would soon follow.

In keeping with the Janissaries' master plan, Cavus Hamza was promoted to the position of guard within the Sultan's retinue. After ten years of patience and plotting, Hamza's moment had finally arrived. On May twenty-ninth, before leaving the palace for the day, he stealthily unlocked several doors. In a celebratory mood after accomplishing the first step of his mission, he reserved his favorite boy at a local pleasure house. The boy was perfect—a young deaf mute with creamy caramel skin.

Within minutes after Hamza arrived, the boy was on his knees, hands clasped in prayer, smiling up at him with huge, dark, kohl-lined eyes. He liked the boy's masses of long ebony curls and the way they felt on his own naked skin, caressing him without the touch of hands. Sexual acts were difficult for a man who hated the touch of other human beings. Hamza's former encounters were always propelled by his administration of "caresses" with a whip or lash applied to someone else. He had never personally felt a caress of any kind until this ingenious boy provided the simple solution.

Lying down on his back on the cotton mattress, he motioned for the boy to begin. The ritual was familiar, having been performed many times before. The boy knelt by the low bed and began using his hair to slowly stroke his client's prone, naked body. As soon as a sign of arousal appeared, the boy increased the tempo and intensity of the strokes by whipping his head back and forth, harder and harder. The client's member responded, standing at attention and begging to be touched, but the boy did not make the mistake of touching it. He had done that once and paid the painful price of the client's displeasure. Once the boundaries had been clearly established, he was happy to have such an easy client who never strayed from the simple routine he required. He continued teasing with his hair around the erect penis, knowing it would end soon and he could relax in a hot bath. He could see the client's lips moving to form words he neither heard nor cared to understand.

"Yes, slave," Hamza whispered. "Make it very hard for me, and listen closely, for you serve the most powerful man in the palace. The...most...powerful...man," he said pumping his hips rhythmically. "When events have run their course, I will take my rightful place." He breathed heavily and arched his back in pleasure, getting harder and harder. "And *then*," he said, thrusting himself into the boy's hair, "the reward for my years of devotion and service will be paid. The promises that have been made will be fulfilled."

When he could no longer contain himself, he gave the signal and the boy got on all fours turning his naked bottom towards the bed. Hamza stood over him and grasped his own member with both hands, pulling and pumping. "I will make them pay," he growled between clinched teeth. "I will tell those rabid bitches what to do." As he ejaculated onto the boy's back, he hissed, "I...will...be...the Kizlar Agasi."

At the very moment of his release, seventy thousand Janissaries attacked the Topkapi Palace without warning. Individual soldiers let themselves in through the gates and doors Hamza had unlocked, and then opened all of the remaining entrances for the troops. Janissaries swarmed over the palace grounds like ants going after a feast of leftover food. Within minutes, they penetrated the interior, killing anyone who tried to stop them or stood in their path. Brave though the palace guards

were, their numbers were no match for the army of Janissaries.

A dozen of Nakshidil's personal guards gathered in
a tight circle around her person, swords in each hand,
preparing to die in her defense.

"Where is my son?" she asked in a panic. Her eyes
searched the room, but she did not see Zahar or any of
her other servants.

"In his quarters being protected as you are, majesty," the head guard replied.

Screams of men and women could be heard above
the unfamiliar sounds of fighting coming from within
the palace. Swords clashed as glass and crockery shattered, bodies slammed into walls and into each other.
Aimée had never heard chaos of this magnitude and
tried hard to organize her thoughts amidst the commotion, but pandemonium ruled. She stood motionless
within the circle of men, completely covered from head
to toe in a sapphire-blue ferace, her mind and heart rac-
ing and the sound of her own blood beating in her ears
like a bass drum.

"Where is the Sultan?" she asked helplessly.

"We have no way to know, Your Grace," he said.

"We must be sure he is safe," she whispered.

"Forgive me, Your Grace, but we cannot leave you
now."

She was helpless and could do nothing for either
Selim or Mahmud. Attempting to calm the panic that
brought a taste like metal into her mouth, she slowly
unwound the rosary beads wrapped around her wrist
and began praying to the Blessed Virgin.

"Holy Mother, full of grace, please find it in your heart to protect those I love. Please keep them safe from harm, I beseech you. If God demands a soul be taken, let it be mine, not theirs."

She recited the rosary quietly to herself with all of the intent and focus she could muster, hoping her concentration might drown out the terrible sounds penetrating her walls. Losing all sense of time, five minutes or five hours might have passed when the inner door to her apartments was breached by what appeared to be hundreds of men. They poured through the door like an infestation of rats, screaming and swinging their swords so ferociously she thought they might cut each other to pieces. Her guards fought until they fell, but could not stem the tide of Janissaries, and in just a few moments she stood alone, shaking from head to toe, surrounded by dead men and glad that no one could see her.

The attackers parted, making an aisle through which a man approached. As he did, she quickly replaced the rosary on her wrist.

Without bowing or showing any form of respect, he said, "Nakshidil, Valide Sultana?"

She nodded her head in reply.

He pointed to the floor with his finger the way you would motion to an obedient dog. "Follow behind me," he said. He turned and walked out of the room, and she followed as instructed.

The halls of the residence were littered with bodies of loyal guards, serving women, and a few Janissaries. As they walked, the soldiers shoved the bodies aside with their feet so they could pass. The smell of fresh blood, feces and urine filled the air, and she held her nostrils closed to breathe only through her mouth, trying frantically to identify what fallen bodies she could, hoping not to recognize anyone but recognizing most. Neither Perestu nor her son was amongst them, and she allowed herself a ray of hope for their safety.

Surrounded by the pack of soldiers, she walked through the halls leading to the seraglio, and suddenly felt a new fear. *What if they mean to enter the harem?* Her mind began skipping forward to a myriad of horrible possibilities—rape, desecration, murder, torture. She was so distraught she found it difficult to breathe.

They stopped in front of the large double doors leading into the women's quarters. Bodies of guards were piled almost to her waist blocking the doors.

She found enough of her voice to say quietly, "Haram."

The soldier turned to look at her and made a snorting sound. "Not for you it isn't," he responded. He barked a command at the soldiers, who began lifting the bodies and moving them aside to free the door. He stood aside and jerked the door open. With a mocking bow and sweep of his arm he ushered her in, saying, "Back to where you started, eh?"

She stepped into the courtyard surrounded by three-story residences as the door closed with a loud bang. No women were present. "Ladies," she called in a quavering voice, "It is I, Nakshidil Sultana." She wanted to crumple onto the floor and wail, but would not allow herself that luxury. The women were hiding and must feel petrified with fear. It was her duty to calm them, to reassure them that all would be well. But would it? How could anything be well again when everything was already lost—or she would not be standing here like this? She slowly removed her ferace.

"Namay?" Perestu's frightened voice whispered.

"Yes, little bird, where are you?"

The young woman emerged from the shadows of an archway, accompanied by a young Indian girl with a bandaged arm. "Namay," she said again as the women hugged each other. "I was coming to visit Sita, who slipped in the bath and hurt her wrist."

"Mahmud, Selim?" Aimée asked.

"Selim, I saw them take him," she sobbed.

"But they did not kill him?"

"No, they took him."

"Where?"

"I do not know."

"Thank God he is alive. And Mahmud?"

"I do not know, Namay. I did not see him."

Other women began to cautiously appear, all asking questions at once: "What happened?"

"Who is doing this and what did they do?"

"We heard screams. Natanya is missing, and Gala and Shira."

"Mikayella, where is Mika?" someone wailed.

Women began running into the courtyard from the baths where they had hidden, some of them naked and wrapped only in towels. What appeared to be about a hundred women all spoke at once, many crying and some too stunned to speak at all.

Nakshidil raised her arms, trying to appear calm

and strong to quiet the hysterical women. "Ladies, please compose yourselves, and I will tell you what I know, which is very little at present. The Janissaries somehow managed to breach the palace and overwhelm our guards. There are thousands of them." Several women began to wail, and she had to raise her voice to quiet them again. "But they did not break the laws of haram—they dare not—and we are safe here. We must wait until someone is able to bring us word. Where is the Kizlar Agasi?"

No one knew the answer to that question yet.

It had been difficult for Nakshidil to find writing paper, pen and ink in the seraglio, as most of the women neither wrote nor read and none corresponded with the outside world. After several days she found enough of everything to finally compose a plea for help. When it was written, she gave it to a trusted serving woman in the main kitchen. "It is the most important message I have ever sent," she said. "All our lives depend on its safe delivery. You must find a way."

"Fear not, your grace. I will not fail you," the woman replied.

June 5, 1807

Dearest Baba,

I pray that these will not be the last words I ever write and that they find their way into your hands. If you are unable to speed with haste to our rescue (again) all will be lost—my son, the Sultan, the Empire and I.

The palace has been seized by thousands of Janissaries,

who slaughtered our people—guards, servants, cooks and eunuchs. I do not know how many, nor how many may have perished outside our walls. Mahmud and I are held like prisoners within the seraglio among the Sultan's women. Why the soldiers did not harm or molest us, or what they intend, we do not know. The Sultan has been put into the Cage.

It grieves me terribly to tell you that following the horrific debacle, the body of our old friend, the Kizlar Agasi, was found close to the harem doors. He had been run through with many swords, no doubt trying to protect the women in his care. Many of the other eunuchs were found in similar states, and there are only twenty here with us.

Thus far, we have gained little information from the outside and can only surmise that the Sultan's army must have been defeated. Perhaps they were simply overrun by the sheer numbers of Janissaries, and I know not of our ships, which sat at the ready in our harbor. Is it to be more terrifying once we learn our fate?

We know that Mustapha sits on the throne, God help us all.

We are sending letters to all of the others who have pledged their fealty to us. I dare not say their names, in the event this should fall into enemy hands. I fear we are at war. The only connection to the outside rests with the tradesmen who are permitted access to us lest we starve. You can imagine how terrified they are made to feel should they help us in any other way.

I hope the messengers, riders and ships are still in place to deliver this to you and that you come to our aid quickly. Please, learn what you can, send word and come quickly, I beg.

Chapter 18

On May thirtieth, after witnessing the onset of a bloody revolution, the French Ambassador, Baron Sébastiani and his wife, Fanny, fled Istanbul to sail for France. Most of the French officers who had been training Turkish troops, along with those overseeing the production of cannon and munitions, also left. Having survived the revolution in their own country, they had no desire to become embroiled in another foreign one, on foreign soil.

As they watched the glistening dome of the Blue Mosque catch the rays of the rising sun and get smaller and smaller, Fanny placed her hand over her husband's and looked up into his eyes. "Will they kill her?" she asked.

"The Valide?"

She nodded. "Yes, Nakshidil. Will they?"

"Most likely," he said. "I am sorry. I know how fond of her you are."

"I was about to say how barbaric they are, but then I remembered *our* bloody revolution, our heads falling." She sighed deeply. "Why does the world have to be so horrid?"

"The price of freedom, my dear, and France is better off as a result," he said. "Bloodshed has always been the currency of change, I'm afraid."

"I suppose they will also kill the Sultan," she said bitterly.

"He is most likely already dead and the new one on the throne."

"Isn't he the terrible young man we heard such horrid stories about?"

"Yes, Mustapha. The Sultans have a long history of insanity, you know. Many of them were quite mad. It's no wonder, being raised in a cage like an animal. I was told the story of one Sultan Ibrahim, who had been put into the Cage at the age of two. Twenty years later, after having no education or human contact of any kind, he was put on the throne. One day, he became angry at his wives...based on a rumor of infidelity they say. He ordered all the wives to be bound and wrapped individually in burlap sacks weighted at the bottom. Then he loaded them onto boats that sailed out into the Bosporus and had them simultaneously thrown into the sea."

Fanny gasped and covered her mouth with her hand.

"Two hundred and eighty women," he said.

She shook her head.

"Some said it was done because he was curious about what kind of sound a hundred drowning women might make. One woman actually escaped from the sack and was rescued by a passing boat bound for France. She told the whole story to the passengers, many of whom refused to believe its veracity."

"Surely, this did not happen in recent years," Fanny said.

"No, about one hundred fifty years ago. It was confirmed by a diver a few days after the event and the Sultan was put back into the cage and replaced by his seven year old son. He entered history as Ibrahim the Deranged."

"What a terrible story," Fanny said. "I can hardly believe it."

"Extraordinary that Sultan Selim was not immured. No doubt that explains his reasonable and civil disposition. It's a shame, really. He was finally putting the Turks on a forward path."

"What will happen now?" she asked.

"God only knows what that madman will do. It is why we are leaving in such haste."

Baron Sébastiani was right on one count and wrong on another: Mustapha sat on the throne less than twenty-four hours after the attack, but he had not killed Selim. Instead, at the Ulema's insistence, he imprisoned Selim in the Cage and allowed Mahmud to remain with his mother in the seraglio.

Mustapha's second official act should have been to honor his mother and proclaim her Valide Sultana, the position for which she had connived, fought and murdered. But no one could *make him* do anything ever again, and his hatred was greater than any sense of responsibility he should have felt. He was finally free of her, of the palace of dreadful women, the Cage, and of everything and everyone who caused him unbearable pain. Reveling in his newfound power, he did not even bother to send word to Nuket Seza. Instead, he began to plot his revenge against them all. But first, he wanted to sample the former Sultan's odalisques, three and four at a time. Orchestrating that was the Valide's task and the reason he allowed her to live.

Sultan Mustapha's newly discovered lust appeared to be unquenchable. He sent requests for women to the Valide all day and into the early hours of the morning. His demands provided great activity for the harem women and gave them a sense of purpose. Hoping to attain positions of favor, they overlooked his lack of appeal and brutish personality. They spent their days primping and preparing, hoping to be chosen. When they were, they bore their welts and bruises proudly, and none yet suffered broken bones or anything worse. If a beating was part of the cost of gaining status, which would mean a private apartment, jewels and an income, most were willing to pay.

The new Sultan spent almost no time on anything else, just as the Ulema intended. They never wished him to actually govern. In fact, they carefully prevented his meddling in any affairs of state. With his attention limited to immediate surroundings, no notice would be paid anywhere else and the priests could run things unimpeded.

Without a Kizlar Agasi, management of the seraglio fell to Nakshidil, and she dared not make any requests, afraid to anger Mustapha or make him feel chastened. Instead, she made do with what was available. Deliveries of food to the seraglio kitchens and bathing necessities to the hamams continued fairly regularly and through those purveyors, she was able to obtain most of what she required. Knowing Mustapha's mercurial and capricious nature kept her on her guard, and she did not know if his hands-off attitude toward her might change. She prayed fervently it would not.

Selim's previously "favored" odalisques now belonged to the new Sultan. The only exempted women were bath servants and serving women, most of whom were too old to be of interest to Mustapha anyway. Both Perestu and Besma, Mahmud's lover, were among these lucky few. Nakshidil hoped that no one would reveal their relationships with her son and the Sultan, lest he summon them out of spite. Fortunately, new girls began to arrive every week to provide a constant distraction.

Five weeks after the debacle, Nakshidil was told that a new Kizlar Agasi would arrive the following day. What the message failed to convey was that the man lacked the most important requirement of that position. He was a white eunuch, which meant his testicles had been taken, but his penis remained intact. His name was Cavus Hamza.

Upon his arrival, the women instantly became obsessed for the new Kizlar Agasi was not only intact, he was young and strong and posed no risk of an unwanted pregnancy. The odalisques literally threw themselves at his feet and Nakshidil's new task became the aversion of disasters created by having a functional yet sterile man in the harem. The dichotomy of the situation was classic—the wolf guarding the sheep. However, this wolf showed little interest in the Sultan's women for any purpose other than punishment.

Throughout the summer and fall, very few written or spoken communications found their way into the seraglio. No responses had been received from any of Sultan Selim's supporters, and Nakshidil had no way of knowing whether her pleas for help had ever been received. In the third week of November, a letter finally broke the silence. Perestu delivered it wrapped in a silk napkin on a tray of coffee and sweets. Nakshidil opened and read it alone in her room by the light of an oil lamp. It was dated ten weeks earlier.

September 3, 1807

To Her Most Gracious Valide Sultana, Nakshidil Sultana, Mother of the Heir, Keeper of the House, Guardian of the Sultan's Women, Benefactress of the Poor, Mother of All Orphans and Exemplar of All That Is Good,

I greet you and wish upon you good health and abundance in all things. May your sorrows also be mine.

It is with a heavy heart I answer your most recent letter and your plea for my aid. Without a moment's hesitation, my ships and my men speed to your side. They sail on the morning's tide. I, however, shall not bask in the comfort of your divine presence nor listen with delight to your melodious voice. All the stamina of my youth, which now seems to have been spent so carelessly, has fled this ancient vessel and try as I might to rally, my flesh and bones will not respond. Alas, I am forced to accept the truth that my old body has retired from its service of me and my anger towards its imposed rest appears useless.

As you know, I am fortunate to have nine capable sons,

each a captain of his own ship, and fifty more ships as well. They rush to your side with all the speed of the righteous wind in their sails. They are my steadfast enforcers now, my stalwart and capable arms, legs and eyes, and they carry with them the fierce purpose of my youth. They are Sultan Selim's to command and shall fight to their deaths for the Empire and for you. If you are reading these words, they are already moored within striking distance of Istanbul. I have sent word to all other loyal Pashas throughout the empire, and expect they too will hasten to your aid.

In the unlikely event our valor proves fruitless, and our cause be lost, I beg you, my lady, to avail yourself of their service on your own behalf. Please allow one of my ships to speed you and your son to the safety of my home in Al-Djazāir, and to my side. There is no need for you to suffer the consequence of war and no shame in taking care for your own safety. I beg you to do so if for nothing more than the foolish enterprise of comforting an old friend.

The enclosed gift needs no explanation other than to say that I kept it all these years as a precious memento of an exquisite young woman who captured my heart and who holds it still.

I am and shall always remain, your humble and devoted servant,

Baba Mohammed Ben Osman, Dey of Al-Djazāir

She unfolded the tiny silk packet and her gold cross that was stolen when she had been stolen, fell into her hand. Tears streamed down her cheeks. Her oldest friend was dying and she could not be at his side. How like Baba to couch his plea for her safety within his own wish to see her. He knew her well. She would never put concern for herself before that of someone she loved, or before duty. She held the cross tightly, and wept for everything and everyone she had lost, and for everything she had found and now feared to lose.

When her tears dried, she went to Mahmud and asked him to walk with her in the tiny garden they were allowed to visit. A chill filled the air and their feet crunched fallen dry leaves on the path as they walked. Winter would come soon.

"I received a letter from Baba Ben Osman," she said very quietly.

"Will he come to our aid?" he asked.

"His ships are already here, within striking distance, he says. He waits for the Pasha's armies to arrive, which he says are on their way."

"This is the best news we have received," he said, trying not to show excitement lest they were being observed.

"Yes," she said smiling up at him. "I feel hope for the first time. Now, we must wait, but you must hope also, Mahmud."

"I shall, Mother."

They sat closely together on a cold stone bench. "There is something I never told you," she said. "Something I now believe to be of the utmost significance."

"I am listening," he said.

She leaned in very close to him, almost whispering in his ear. "Long ago, when I was a very young girl, a fortune teller told my whole life to me after seeing it in a pile of tiny bones."

His brows raised and he almost laughed. "You?" he asked.

"Yes, me and my cousin Rose."

"You mean the Empress Josephine?"

"She was not yet an empress at fourteen, but yes. The fortune-teller was an old *obeah* woman, a Creole, part African and part Irish. She said many things, some of which I've forgotten, but she told me about you and spoke of this moment and the things that would lead up to it. They have all occurred."

"Truly?" he asked skeptically. "Everything?"

She nodded her head. "Yes, Mahmud, and the reason I tell you this now is quite important because you are going to be required to do something against your nature, something terrible that under ordinary circumstances neither of us would condone."

He listened and watched her face carefully.

"You will have to commit murder," she said.

A mystified expression crossed his face. "And you condone it? I find that difficult to believe."

"That is precisely why I tell you this now. When the time comes, you must not hesitate. It will be a matter of your life or his—and it must not be yours, Mahmud."

"Do you know whom I will…murder?" he asked.

She nodded her head. "Yes. Shall I tell you?"

It was Mahmud's turn to nod. "Yes, I think so."

"Mustapha."

Chapter 19

It had taken ten months after the Janissaries deposed Selim for Pasha Baicatar from the Provence of Rustchuk to gather fifty thousand troops—an army large enough to march on Istanbul. Leaving his men bivouacked two miles outside the city, the Pasha took a small group of twelve with him to the Topkapi Palace. Outside the exterior gate, he identified himself as a representative of the Ulema who wished to ascertain the well-being of the prisoner Selim. The guards allowed them to pass. Once inside, they approached the seraglio gate and sent a message to Sultan Mustapha reiterating the same request and adding a reminder that it was made according to the edicts of the Ulema.

Angered by the audacity of an insignificant Pasha to make a demand of *him*, Mustapha ignored the request and summoned a henchman instead.

Moments later, Cavus Hamza, the new Kizlar Agasi, walked boldly up to the ornate curtain that hid the throne where the Sultan sat. He cleared his throat quietly to let the monarch know he was present. A hand appeared at the far edge of the curtain, and a high-pitched voice barked out a command. Two servants pulled the curtain aside revealing an enormously fat young man completely draped in gold cloth and jewels, reclining on silk cushions.

"Who are you?" the Sultan squeaked rudely.

"I am the Kizlar Agasi, Cavus Hamza," he replied with a deep bow.

"On your knees, slave!" he barked, and several guards pushed Hamza to his knees.

"You summoned me, Sire," he said without lifting his eyes from the floor.

Mustapha lifted his right arm to order the pompous slave's murder when he suddenly remembered who he was. "Are you the assassin?" he asked.

"Yes, Sire."

"You should have said so. I want you to kill them both...now, right away."

"Yes, Sire, the former Sultan and...?"

"And the Heir, of course, you stupid wretch! I am to be the only Ottoman...the only Sultan...I am! Me, Sultan Mustapha." He settled himself back into the cushions. "Unnerstan'?" he asked, leaning forward.

"Yes, of course, Sire, I understand."

"Bring Arak!" the Sultan shouted to no one in particular. "And be quick about it now." His voice trailed off and he seemed to lose focus or interest. "I need my medicine. Bring my gold pills, the big ones," he whined. "Close the curtain!" he screamed at the top of his voice. From behind the curtain he added, "Bring the bodies here to me."

Hamza backed out of the throne room, keeping his eyes on the curtain and on the guards. The unstable sultan might change his mind at any moment and shout a command to kill him, as he had almost done moments ago. *One day,* he thought as he made his way down the hallway, *I would like very much to silence that annoying voice.*

~ ~ ~

The deaf mute guards who served the Cage had their own means of communication. It was a system that had been developed long ago and passed on for hundreds of years. No one knew of its existence save their own kind. They used their hands. Looking directly at one another, they made signs in the air and in their palms with their fingers. In this way, they could pass on information, share opinions and make requests. They were able to "discuss" those in their care, and none of them had anything bad to say about Selim. In fact, they admired him. Immediately upon his arrival, he observed their method of "talking" and understood that they were deaf and mute, but not dumb.

Selim invented his own method to summon them to his door. His cell did not have windows low enough for anyone to see through, and the deaf guards could not hear his voice. So he used his balled fists pounding on the door to create vibrations the guards were able to sense and feel. Three consecutive thumps meant he needed water, and two meant food. He had even asked to learn their signs for those items.

Observing a strong resemblance between two of his

guards, Selim discovered that they were indeed twins. He wondered if their unique connection heightened their ability to communicate with thoughts, or perhaps their inability to hear and speak allowed other senses to develop more acutely. Whatever the source, their quick intelligence was immediately obvious to Selim, and he offered to teach them to read and write. This is how he eventually learned their names—Sala and Havi.

No one had ever shown them kindness or interest and *his* interest in them caused them to make an effort to know him. Due to their respect for the imprisoned sultan and the congeniality of their relationship, they allowed Nakshidil to visit regularly. She brought books, paper, pen and ink—everyday items that helped Selim to pass the time and enlighten the guards. Although completely covered by her ferace, they liked the way she smelled and the feel of her soft touch when she laid her hand upon their arms. Her touch evoked vague memories of something they remembered liking but did not understand. Like all deaf mutes, they had been taken from their mother as soon as they were identified.

Sala was on duty that afternoon when a man, dressed in simple dark trousers and tunic with soft kidskin boots, approached the exterior door of the Cage. He signaled the guard to open the door and stepped into the dim interior as the door closed behind him. He waited several minutes for his eyes to adjust. He knew there were only two guards inside, and they were on duty one at a time. One of them stood in front of the prisoner's door with a sword in one hand and a curved knife tucked into the front of his waist sash. When his vision had acclimated, Cavus Hamza made a deep bow and at the lowest point, carefully retrieved a small knife from the top of his soft boot. In one swift motion he rose, letting the knife fly, and lunged towards the guard. The small knife found its mark in the guard's throat and before he could react in his own defense, another plunged into his heart. Hamza held onto the body until it was still, then allowed it to slip quietly to the floor. After removing his blades, he took the cell door key from the dead guard's belt and unlocked the door.

The former Sultan sat facing the door on an odd-looking piece of furniture on the opposite side of the room, and instantly stood. He felt no need to ask the intruder who he was. It did not matter. There was only one reason for him to be there.

"Do infidels pray to Allah?" Hamza asked.

"I have no way to know the answer to that," Selim replied, "but I do."

"Then I will allow you a moment to fall onto your knees and do so."

"I have no need to pray at this moment," Selim said.

"You must have lived an exemplary life," Hamza said.

"Allah is great, and I am his servant."

Hamza could tell that this man was not going to be easy to kill. Keeping his eyes on Selim, he began to move slowly to his left, and Selim mimicked his movement. The two began moving clockwise around the room, their backs to the wall. When Selim had almost reached the open doorway, the other deaf mute guard stepped through it, over the body of his dead brother with his sword and knife drawn. For an instant, Selim thought he was going to be run through, but the guard nodded his head once to Selim and handed him the short blade. He thought he saw the hint of a tear slide down the guard's cheek as the two faced off together against Hamza. Following the guard's lead, they slowly advanced forward. Selim could see the fear on the assassin's face that he was not a brave man, but a bully. The realization gave Selim courage, and he roared like an ancient warrior as he lunged toward his opponent, stabbing upward into his jugular. Sensing Selim's intention, Havi instantly attacked from the other side. Hamza collapsed with blood gushing out of two wounds—one in his neck, and one in his heart.

Knowing there was no time to waste, Selim scribbled three words on a small piece of paper, folded it and wrote the word, "Valide." He put it into the hand of the guard, who nodded his understanding and secreted the paper within his girdle. The two men ran from the room and stopped at the outer door of the Cage, where the guard knocked the signal for opening, and backed away with his sword drawn. As the door opened, the outer guard saw Selim first and instinctively thrust his sword forward, piercing him through the heart. The former Sultan died instantly and crumpled to the ground. Havi, pretending he had been pursuing the prisoner, patted the guard's shoulder and signaled he would go to alert those in command. Then he continued forward toward the seraglio. To avoid other guards, he moved cautiously to the side entrance used by purveyors, and made his way into the kitchens. No one paid much attention to the deaf mute. He stopped at the door that led to a hallway in the seraglio, knowing he would not be allowed to continue any further, and looked around the busy kitchen until he saw an older serving woman—the one the Valide used to get messages to and from Selim. Havi knew that she too knew how to read. He walked up to her and showed her the folded piece of paper. When she saw the word "Valide" she nodded and quickly secreted the paper in her girdle. Havi held her wrist tightly and looked straight into her eyes, letting her know how important it was that this be delivered safely. She nodded again, then picked up a dish of almond-stuffed dates and walked through the door into the seraglio.

In less than one minute, the serving woman stood before the Valide and handed her the note. When Nakshidil opened it she read, "Assassins. Save Mahmud." She squeezed the woman's hand in thanks and ran to Mahmud's rooms.

Thrusting the paper into his hands, she said, "Hide."

"Who sent this?" he asked.

"Selim."

She wrapped the dates in a napkin and thrust them into his hands with a bottle of water. "Go now and hide until you are sure it is safe."

"The old chimney," he said to her as he ran out the door.

Nakshidil's heart was beating wildly, yet she felt frozen to the spot where she stood. She tried to calm her thoughts by inhaling deeply through her nostrils and slowly exhaling. In a few minutes her mind felt clearer, and she was able to walk to a chair and sit. She stood up again and walked to the door, calling for Perestu. Then she sat back down and began to organize her thoughts.

Perestu appeared in the doorway. "What's wrong?" she asked as soon as she saw Nakshidil's face.

"Come in," she said as calmly as she could.

"Satya brought me this," she said, handing her the little piece of paper.

The young woman's eyes widened. "Who wrote it?"

"It came from Selim."

"How?"

"I do not know, but Mahmud is gone...in hiding, and you must say nothing to anyone. You know nothing."

Perestu nodded and handed the paper back to Nakshidil, who dropped it into the charcoal brazier that burned next to her chair. It flamed brightly for a moment, turned into ash and then disappeared. She frantically searched her mind trying to think of someone she could turn to for help, but could think of no one; the old Kizlar Agasi was gone, so was the Kadine, and Selim was in the Cage. She rose out of the chair at the thought.

"I must go see Selim," she said. "Wait here, little bird. Do not leave these rooms."

She had not gone more than ten steps in the courtyard when twenty or more women came screaming through the entrance to one of the baths. "Soldiers, soldiers, through the gates," they screamed.

"What soldiers, where?"

"Everywhere," they yelled, and chaos ensued in the harem, women running into and out of all the rooms.

Nakshidil pounded her fists on the inside of the

locked doors of the main entrance to the seraglio. "I am the Valide and wish to speak with the Kizlar Agasi," she called.

"The Kizlar Agasi is not here," came the reply.

"Then I wish to speak with the captain of the guards," she said.

There was a commotion outside the doors, and a moment later they opened wide. A battalion of men stood outside the doors, but they were not Janissaries. Nakshidil realized that she was not covered, and the men instinctively turned their faces from her. A large, older man made his way through the crowd and stood before her. "Valide," he said with a deep bow. "If you wish to retrieve your ferace, I will await."

"I care nothing for protocol at this moment, sir. Please tell me who you are."

"Pasha Baicatar, your grace, beneficent ruler of the Provence of Rustchuk and loyal servant of the true Sultan, Selim, at your service."

She breathed a sigh of relief. "And Baba Ben Osman?" she asked.

"I serve in his name, your grace."

"Thank you, sir," she said. "Thank God you've arrived. Where is Selim?"

"We are here to find out," he replied, "on our way to demand Mustapha grant us a meeting. I will leave my guards posted at these doors and will return with word when we have met with him. Please remain within, Your Grace."

Aimée nodded and stepped back into the courtyard as the heavy doors closed.

~ ~ ~

The Pasha and half of his men were shown into one of the Sultan's informal reception rooms. The Sultan's throne sat at the far end of the room with the curtain drawn closed. Only four Janissary guards stood against the walls, and one of them said, "Speak your piece."

"I am Pasha Baicatar, ruler of the Provence of Rustchuk, and I formally request an audience with the former Sultan Selim, as the edict of the Ulema provides."

The voice from behind the curtain replied, "The person you speak of is a prisoner. No audience is allowed a prisoner."

"In this case," the Pasha replied, "no audience is actually required. I simply wish to see his person with my own eyes. There is no need for conversation, if my lord does not wish us to speak."

Soft laughter could be heard from behind the curtain. "Very well then. You may see him, as you wish, and I doubt very much he will speak to you. Guards!" he shouted. "Bring the former Sultan before us."

A door behind the throne opened, and two guards dragged the body of Selim into the room and dropped it at the Pasha's feet. "The former Sultan Selim for your viewing," Mustapha said.

The Pasha fell to his knees and held the lifeless face in his hands. "What have you done?" he asked.

One of his men stood close to him and whispered, "Let me kill him now." He pulled the curtain aside to reveal Mustapha reclining there. Simultaneously, the Pasha's men overwhelmed the Janissary guards and dragged the whimpering Sultan onto the floor.

"Stand on your feet!" the Pasha commanded. "You will lead us out of the palace, instructing any guards who may attempt to prevent our exit to stand aside. Do you understand?"

Mustapha cringed and nodded his head, then whimpered, "But you should know that I am the last of the Ottoman blood line." *They dare not kill the last living Ottoman*, he thought.

Pasha Baicatar stood very close to Mustapha. "Where is the heir, Mahmud?" he asked quietly.

Mustapha shrugged his shoulders. "I am not sure where he is, but wherever that may be, he is already dead. You are too late."

"We shall see," the Pasha answered. "Now, lead us out of here and walk directly to the Divan."

The group of men, carrying the lifeless body of Selim and led by the Sultan Mustapha, walked unimpeded through the palace as servants and purveyors scattered away into the shadows.

~ ~ ~

A serving woman burst into the seraglio asking for the Valide. In moments, Nakshidil stood before her. The woman fell to her knees and said breathlessly, "Some Pashas are walking with the Sultan Mustapha towards the Divan. They carry the body of Sultan Selim."

"Is he alive?" she asked.

"I do not think so," the woman answered, and began to weep.

Without hesitation, Nakshidil ran through the secret passageway that led to the "eye of the Sultan," her secret observation room in the Divan. She opened the door quietly and looked down through the latticework into the room where the small group stood. Selim's lifeless body had been laid on a bed of cushions with his arms crossed on his chest. She could not take her eyes from it and bit her lower lip to keep from crying out.

"Please, Sire," Baicatar said, inviting Mustapha to sit on his throne. "Now you will summon your minions and instruct them to find Mahmud and bring him to you...alive. We will wait here until they have done so."

"I am afraid, as I said earlier, that you are too late. I have already sent my men to find Mahmud...and to strangle him." He picked a small bit of dust off his trouser leg, then looked up sullenly. "So, you see, you cannot kill me."

"We shall await his arrival, either way," the Pasha said.

Nakshidil held her breath and pressed both hands over her mouth lest she scream. Selim was dead! She turned and fled the room, running down the passageway as fast as she could, frantically trying to think what Mahmud meant when he said, "the old chimney." *Which old chimney, where?* If they had already found him, he would also be dead.

She ran through the seraglio using the back entrances and little-known passageways used mostly for secret assignations—*and treason*, she thought. She reminded herself to be quiet in case Mustapha's men were looking in the same places. *But they cannot be inside*, she thought, *it is* haram. She entered one of the main bathing areas, and stood still to catch her breath and think. *There is nowhere to hide here except maybe the small servants' rooms.* She searched every tiny room and alcove, but did not find her son. Leaving the *hamam*, she moved quietly down another hallway, trying not to run or cause attention, and slipped into another, smaller bath area. Checking the outer rooms first, she found nothing but the neatly hanging garments belonging to a few women.

Nakshidil tried hard to focus. *Chimneys*, she thought. She had an idea. Leaving the outer room, she looked for the entrance to where the fires that heat the water were stoked—the furnace room. It was one of the few places within the seraglio that she had never been. There had to be a door somewhere that led to stairs beneath the water. She had seen the halberdiers bringing stacks of wood to the entrance from the outside, but where might there be an inside entrance?

She saw a familiar stairway that led up to the roof of the bath and walked towards it. There was a door she had never noticed before, beneath the stairs, which she opened. The odor of old, long-cold fires filled her nostrils, and a dark stairway led down. She had no lamp, and pressed the palms of her hands against the walls on either side of the stairs to carefully descend. There were cobwebs everywhere, indicating the entrance had not been used in a while. Suddenly overcome by a feeling of hopelessness, she sat down and began to cry. "Mahmud, my son," she said sobbing.

"Mother?"

"Mahmud? Is that really you?"

The dark form of a man walked out of the shadows towards her with extended hands. Barely able to see him in the gloom, she grabbed his hands. Feeling his warmth and knowing he was alive, not a ghost, she hugged him and cried. "Mahmud," she said again.

"I hid in the old chimney," he said. "No one ever knew that I'd found it when I was a little boy. It was my secret place."

"Thank God you're alive," she said. "They killed Selim."

"What?" he whispered, holding her at arm's length.

"He is gone, Mahmud."

Grief and anger flooded his body all at once. "Mustapha shall pay for this," he said through clenched teeth.

"Right now, there is no time to grieve," Nakshidil said. "We must learn as much as we can of our situation. There is only a small group of our people here, in the reception room with Mustapha. You must show yourself to them, let them know you are alive. I will go with you through the secret passage."

She followed him up the dark stairs and they made their way back to the "eye of the Sultan."

Chapter 20

Immediately after delivering Selim's message, Havi returned to the Cage. The Sultan's body was gone, but his brother and the assassin still lay where they had fallen. Caring nothing at all for the latter, he knelt beside his brother. Sala had not just been his brother, he had been the only other human being with whom he could communicate—until Selim. He gently touched the expressionless face, the duplicate of his own. Tears filled his eyes and he knew he should alert the captain of the guards, but did not want to leave his brother's side. *What will become of me now, Sala? I avenged your death, but that will not bring you back.* No one else ever heard his thoughts. Filled with grief, he held his brother's body to his own and wept, as his eyes searched the room for something that might ease his pain. He saw the tiny writing table and his heart filled with hope. *I can read and write*, he thought.

He picked his brother's body up and carried him out into the sunlight where he gently laid him down on the soft grass. Then he walked back to the Cage, into the cell that Selim had occupied for almost a year, and sat at the little table where he'd learned the magic of letters.

Picking up the pen, he dipped it into the ink and began to write. When he finished, Havi folded the note and carefully gathered all the pieces of paper on which Selim had written. He put them into the wooden box the Valide had brought, along with the pen and ink, then left the Cage and walked towards the seraglio. Inside the kitchen, he found the old serving woman and handed her the box along with the note that read, "Valide." She looked into his eyes and nodded. Having completed his task, he walked back to where his brother lay and sat next to him to await whatever may come next. There was no longer a need to stand guard on the empty cage.

~ ~ ~

Nakshidil watched from the "eye of the Sultan," as the secret door behind the throne opened and Mahmud appeared. All of the men stopped talking and stared at the soot-covered apparition with bright blue eyes. When it took a step towards them, they raised their swords.

Mahmud slowly brought his hands to his heart in greeting. "I am Mahmud, son of Abdul Hamid," he said evenly.

The Pasha and his men fell to their knees and touched their foreheads to the floor.

"You are not real!" Mustapha screamed. "You are dead...a ghost."

"I assure you," Mahmud replied. "I am quite alive, unlike Sultan Selim, whose death you shall pay for with the forfeiture of your freedom."

"Allow me to take him to the Cage, Sire," one of the men said.

"Please," Mahmud replied. "And stay with him until I release you."

"You cannot," Mustapha said. "You are nothing, no one, you cannot command anyone, you have no power."

Three men picked Mustapha up as he kicked and screamed like an angry child. He continued hurling insults and threats as they carried him out of the room. "My guards will kill you...the Janissaries will slaughter everyone...you will all die and I will put your stinking heads on spikes at the gate!"

The doors closed behind them, silencing his shrill cries.

"Please, Sire," the Pasha said. "Your presence gives us hope. I have fifty thousand men camped outside the city, and Baba Ben Osman's fleet is ready to sail into the harbor at my signal. The people will rally behind you to overthrow Mustapha. Are you prepared to take the throne?"

Mahmud looked up at the latticework walls, knowing his mother watched from above. "I am," he said.

"Please take your seat, your grace," the Pasha said, indicating the raised platform.

Mahmud regarded the platform for a moment and shook his head. "No, I will not sit on that throne. Please bring me the chair Sultan Selim sat upon. It was moved to the anteroom."

Three men left and returned moments later carrying an ornate Empire-style chair.

"Remove that," Mahmud said pointing to platform

Mustapha had been reclining on. "And place the chair there."

It took only moments.

Mahmud addressed the pasha. "The former Sultan Mustapha murdered the rightful Sultan Selim along with thousands of other innocent men, women and children. For these crimes, I demand he be judged by the Ulema. Until that time, he will be held prisoner in the Cage."

"As you command, Sire" the pasha replied.

Mahmud slowly walked to the throne. Standing before it, he closed his eyes and bowed his head in silent prayer. He turned around and slowly sat down.

Nakshidil watched as her son took his rightful place. *At a terrible cost*, she thought. *Selim is dead—the blood that was spilled was his.* She did not allow herself to weep because she knew once she did she might never stop.

The men stood and made their obeisance.

"If I may speak freely, Sire?" the Pasha asked.

"Of course."

"The Sultan may wish to bathe before receiving any other guests."

Mahmud looked down at his blackened robes and smiled. "Thank you, Sir, I believe you are correct."

~ ~ ~

That evening, after moving back into the apartments of the Valide Sultana, Nakshidil allowed herself the luxury of tears. Her lover was gone and the forty days of mourning were about to begin. She was going to need every one of them to come to terms with her loss. The only thing that helped to alleviate her grief was her fear for Mahmud's life.

~ ~ ~

The following morning, she went to visit her son.

"I want to show you something," she said, handing him the carved wooden box containing Selim's writings. "These are Selim's last thoughts, which I know he would want you to have. And there is one other thing—a note written by one of his guards."

"Written?" he asked incredulously.

"Yes, Selim taught him and his twin brother how to write and read. I've no doubt he helped to save your life. Selim's assassin was stabbed by two different blades."

Mahmud read the note written in a child's hand: *Please let me serve the true Sultan Mahmud as I served Sultan Selim. To guard his life with my own. Your faithful, Havi.*

"How extraordinary," Mahmud said. "Is this the man who guards Mustapha in the Cage?"

"That is something you may want to ensure," his mother replied.

"Yes. Right now, I want him as close to Mustapha as possible," he said. "In the future, I will keep him near to me."

~ ~ ~

The Pasha's army wasted no time. Fifty thousand troops marched into Istanbul, as Baba's fleet of ships stood in the harbor nearby. The Janissaries revolted more violently than ever, and a full-scale civil war began. Citizens who wanted Mahmud on the throne now had the military backing of Selim's army. The Janissaries remained determined to reinstate Mustapha.

The fighting took over the streets of Istanbul for almost four months with heavy losses on all sides. Those in favor of Mahmud had one great advantage in Mahmud himself, for he inspired loyalty. Ordinary citizens, happy with modernization, fought to keep what they had gained. The new army was better equipped than the Janissaries, and had the support of the Royal Ottoman Navy. The Janissaries had never encountered such fierce opposition from their own countrymen.

In a final desperate attempt, the Janissaries attacked the Palace again.

~ ~ ~

As the hostile forces attempted to breach the palace walls, Nakshidil pleaded with her son to act. "Mahmud, as the one who brought you into this world, I beg you to heed my words. Mustapha must die. It is *kismet*, my son—it has been written."

Mahmud knew she was right. The Janissaries would never capitulate. The only way to permanently end the bloody struggle for power was to put an end to the choice. He sent an order to Havi to strangle the only remaining heir.

~ ~ ~

Sultan Mustapha IV was buried next to the Hagia Sophia mosque without ceremony, and no one openly observed the official period of mourning.

The Ulema's investigation revealed Cavus Hamza's identity as a Janissary spy and clearly implicated the Janissaries in Sultan Selim's death. As the intricate web of intrigue, lies and crimes began to unravel, Hamza's role in the death of the Circassian Kadine also came to light. The Janissaries would be held accountable for their participation in both murders, and those responsible would be sentenced to death by hanging. In response to the irrefutable evidence, the Ulema cut all remaining ties of that alliance and gave their full support to Sultan Mahmud.

The immediate threat of the Janissaries had been eliminated, yet they remained. In a private meeting with his trusted advisors, Sultan Mahmud asked, "What do you recommend we do with the deceitful, untrustworthy lot of them?"

"We cannot simply abolish the Janissaries," one man said. "It is not within our power. I've no idea how we might rein them in. Many have attempted to do so in the past, to no avail. There are forty thousand, and they are armed."

"Have you no suggestions?" the Sultan asked.

"May we discuss this further amongst ourselves?" the advisor responded.

"By all means. But please know that I will put an

end to their murderous acts and sedition. The Janissaries may survive, but hear me well, their rule is over from this day forward."

Chapter 21

Chilling winds swept off the Seine and rattled the tall glass windows in the formal dining room of the Emperor and Empress of France. They dined alone at the ornately carved olivewood table, an unusual occurrence suggested by Napoleon that Josephine duly noted. They had not discussed the bastard son of his mistress for months, and now all of France knew of his existence. Citizens argued the topic of a royal heir in cafés, and newspaper editorials boldly suggested divorce. It seemed that every French citizen, including the Emperor, wanted an heir.

"Will you submit to their demands?" Josephine asked.

"I fear I must, my dear. My duty is to the Empire, and she requires an heir."

She was about to say, "And what of your duty to me?" but instantly realized how foolish it would sound to put herself on the same footing as the Empire. Instead she said, "Do our marriage vows mean so little to you?"

"They mean the world to me, as do you, but they do

not preclude my responsibility as an Emperor. As the Empress, surely, you cannot disagree with that."

"How difficult it must be to choose your country above your heart," she said sarcastically.

"Unfortunately, my heart lies with both. Please try to understand that I am asking for your compliance in this. The people also love you, and I would not turn away from you or dismiss you for any sake—even though I may be legally sworn to another."

She rose angrily from her chair in a sudden motion, causing it to fall loudly to the floor. Three servants came running in and, heedless of their presence, she began a furious tirade. "You fear the people will turn from you because they love *me!*" she screamed. "They love me because I am one of them, not an outsider, a foreigner whom they do not fully trust. Wasn't that why you married me—and now you want my compliance in my own divorce?"

Overcome with emotion, she found herself having difficulty breathing. She leaned forward on the table to steady herself, and all the color drained out of her face as she fainted.

Dearest cousin Aimée,

I enclose herewith two letters written to you with no way to post. I held them hoping a way would present itself, and so it has in the person of our Minister of Oriental Trade. I have added the more recent musings at the end.

September 1, 1807

I was desperate to receive news of you from Baron Sébastiani upon his return to Paris, and horrified to learn of the events that led to the Sultan's imprisonment. I hoped and prayed that you and your son were safe and, thankfully, received confirmation of this by subsequent reports. Still, I know little of the actual details, only that which the fleeing officers brought with them. Most importantly, I know you are both safe. Please write to enlighten me if you are able.

Your loving cousin,

Rose

March 21, 1808

Dearest cousin,

War again threatens our beloved France, this time at the behest of my husband. He has taken Spain and plans to put his brother Joseph on the throne. It appears our Empire is not yet large enough to suit his need.

My circumstance has also become jeopardized, perhaps not as desperately as yours. My inability to produce an heir has driven a wedge between my husband and me. Beyond that, it has also caused an extraordinary "call to arms" among citizens. It pains him greatly to put country before me, but this is what his duty and our people now demand. They and he wish to see the continuance of Empire through his bloodline of sons, sons I shall never bear. He has asked me to acquiesce fully in this matter and assured me that my title and position will not be changed. It causes us both much aggravation and grief. Now he must discern how to extricate himself. This may not be easy, as two years ago he foolishly enacted a statute within an imperial decree forbidding divorce for members of the imperial family. His advisors and solicitors ponder this daily, and I am sure will eventually discover a useful ambiguity.

As to whether or not the Holy Father may be willing to grant divorce, we do not know. Few men have ever refused my husband anything and so, this too shall most likely come to pass.

I remain as ever, your devoted cousin,
Rose

PS The search for my successor now begins in earnest with inquiries to Czar Alexander and the Russian royal family. Please answer as soon as you are able with any advice regarding my newly proposed status. I suspect your position within the realm of the Ottomans may have produced some wisdom regarding marital relations of which I am unaware. My heart aches and I find no solace in anything. I have always tried to erase the memory of Madame David's last words to me but they are all I think of now. I have indeed "astonished the world" and shall now "die alone and miserable."

Josephine found no hope for her marriage in the year that followed, as pressure for an imperial heir increased. Napoleon strengthened his resolve, and in the fall of 1809, a new window of opportunity opened with the proposal of annulment rather than divorce. This solved three tricky issues: it eliminated the need for the sanction of the Holy Father, did not contradict the stipulation of the Imperial edict, and appeased the Czar's objections, on religious grounds, of a proposed marriage with that house. Even Josephine could no longer use the excuse of religion to object. Assured of keeping her title, income and position, Josephine agreed.

On December 15, 1809 the dissolution of the civil marriage began with Napoleon and Josephine's statements read by Eugène de Beauharnais at a formal hearing in Paris.

The Emperor said, *"God knows what such a decision has cost to my heart! But there is no sacrifice that is beyond my courage if it is shown to be for the good of France. I must add that, far from having any reason for reproach, I have nothing but praise for the attachment and the affection of my beloved wife: she has graced fifteen years of my life; the memory of them will remain engraved in my heart. She was crowned by my hand; I desire that she retain the rank and title of crowned Empress, but more than this, that she never doubt my feelings and that she value me as her best and dearest friend."*

The Empress Josephine replied, *With our most august and dear husband's permission, I must declare that, no longer holding out any hope for a child that could satisfy both his political needs and the good of France, I give to him the greatest proof of attachment and devotion that has ever been given on this earth. Everything I have comes from his greatness; it is his hand that crowned me, and upon this throne, I have received evidence of nothing but affection and love from the French people.*

I acknowledge these feelings in agreeing to the dissolution of this marriage, which from this moment on is an obstruction to the well-being of France, depriving it from the joy of one day being governed by the descendants of a great man clearly chosen by Providence to eradicate the evils of a terrible revolu-

tion and re-establish the altar, the throne and social order. Nevertheless, the dissolution of my marriage will change nothing of the feelings in my heart: the Emperor will have in me always his greatest friend. I know how much this act, called for by politics and greater interests, has pained his heart; but glorious is the sacrifice that he and I make for the good of our nation.

Nakshidil read the verbatim statements of the Emperor and Empress published in her own French newspaper, and wept. When she read Napoleon's words "the memory of them will remain engraved in my heart," she had to set the paper down. It was odd to see the French translation of her own name, attached to her dearest cousin, Rose. She immediately went to her writing table.

March 1, 1810

Dearest, dearest cousin,

Despite the many sorrows you endure, despite the loss and pain, you will always remain the most inspiring example of womanhood. You are kind, beautiful, gracious and filled with joie de vivre! Your light has shown at the very center of one of the greatest Empires in the world, and no one can ever take that glory from you.

When I was lost at sea, I held on to the image of the young man I had grown so fond of during that voyage, Mr. Angus Braugham. My feelings for him guided me through those first frightening weeks. I placed all my hope for rescue upon him. Yet, rescue came instead from a stranger I first thought of as barbarian.

You, my dear cousin, still have so many people to give

you hope. Your children, grandchildren and the whole of France adore you. Allow them to heal your wounded heart and heed your husband's proclamation of his love for you. You are now and shall always be a queen. More importantly, you are surrounded by those who love you.

We are no longer young women looking towards future happiness—no longer Yeyette and Maymay. Instead, we must take comfort in those gifts we have been given.

Do not despair, dear cousin, for you are beloved.

I remain as ever your loving cousin,

Aimée

~ ~ ~

On March 11, 1810, two months after the annulment was finalized, Napoleon wed by proxy nineteen-year-old Archduchess Marie-Louise of Austria. Separate secular and religious ceremonies followed on April first and second. The bride's royal pedigree was impeccable—she belonged to the House of Habsburg, a family that had ruled Switzerland and Austria for over three hundred years. Her father, Francis II, was Holy Roman Emperor, and her mother, Maria Theresa of Naples-Sicily, the niece of Marie-Antoinette. Unfortunately, Napoleon's invasion had forced the young Marie-Louise and her family to flee their homeland. The resulting hatred of the man they called "the ugly dwarf" was permanently instilled. Napoleon's second marriage was made out of war, unlike his union with Josephine, which had come out of passion. Napoleon's threat of invasion had prompted Emperor Francis's consent to the marriage.

Napoleon attempted to assuage his new wife's fear of him by attentiveness and deference. He devoted the first weeks of their union solely to her happiness, rarely leaving her side. Despite his efforts, Marie-Louise was unable to do anything more than stoically tolerate the man she thought of as her conqueror. To her, the union was an obligation to her family and country. Enjoyment and affection were not mandated within the same sense of duty, and this quickly became clear to her husband. He had indeed "married a womb," as Josephine said.

Exactly one month after the royal marriage, on May 10, Countess Marie Lontchinska, Napoleon's Polish mistress, gave birth to his second bastard son, Alexandre-Florian-Joseph, upon whom Napoleon conferred the title Comte Colonna Walewski.

The birth seemed to bolster the Emperor's confidence, or perhaps the frustration of an unhappy marriage gave rise to need. Whatever the cause, something inspired Napoleon's renewed determination to bring Great Britain to its knees. For six years, France had demanded compliance of the trade embargo against Great Britain from its allies Russia, Prussia, Spain, Holland, Austria and Portugal. War had been declared on Spain and Portugal when they failed to comply. However, the embargo proved to be a burden on all countries involved as it severely hampered their import and export trade. So, some countries began to relax their enforcements. In response, Napoleon demanded more funds and ships to enforce the blockade. When his own brother, Louis, King of Holland, refused to divert funds that would throw his country into bankruptcy, Napoleon forced him to abdicate. This prompted the kings of five other countries to ask, "If Napoleon disempowers and exiles his own brother, what might he do to us?" The scales began to tip.

Chapter 22

The former Empress Josephine Bonaparte sat in Mlle. Le Normand's salon, sipping a cup of strong black tea. The decor of the small room was a bizarre blend of Empire, Oriental and the newest French avant-garde, with heavy velvet drapes shutting out all outside light. The dim glow from kerosene lamps and rococo candelabras gave the room a soft, dreamlike quality.

Josephine removed her hat. Her dark hair, once described as "raven" was now heavily peppered with grey and gathered into a small knot at the base of her neck. Her shoulders and chest appeared shrunken beneath her fashionable yet slightly worn dress that, like her hair, had lost the clarity of its original color. Fine lines creased her once flawless complexion like an old map, and the dimness of the room accentuated the hollows beneath her eyes. She wore her unhappiness as plainly as she wore her old clothes.

Mlle. Le Normand reclined comfortably on a red velvet settee, languidly fanning herself with a large, white ostrich-plume fan. Her artificially enhanced red hair was piled high in curly mounds atop her cherubic face. The plump whiteness of her skin against the brightness of her painted lips seemed to exaggerate her guest's' unhealthy appearance. As the spiritualist spoke, one chubby little hand slowly twirled the ropes of crystal beads that graced her ample bosom.

"Has the birth of a legitimate heir brought his Highness what he wished for?" she asked.

"In part," Josephine replied. "He adores the boy, who he says looks just like him. But his bride spurns him as her country's oppressor. He chose her for political gain and royal lineage. Now that she has fulfilled her duty, she longs to escape his grasp."

"Truly?" the older woman asked. "I suppose it makes sense. Love would not easily follow invasion. But tell me of you, dear. How do you fare at Malmaison? We miss you so, here in Paris."

"Thank you, Mademoiselle, I miss Paris as well. Napoleon still writes me daily of all the news. He does not wish me to want for anything, and has been extremely generous. He is encouraging me to visit Aix to take the waters. As you can see, I have not felt well of late."

"I am glad to hear of his concern, Madame, and perhaps the Emperor is correct. The waters will put the roses back in your cheeks."

"Yes, I may take a short trip there soon, and plan an extended stay for early spring and summer."

"I am very glad to learn he has not cast you aside."

"Oh no. He continues to assure me of his affections—within the bounds of propriety of course," she added. *I must be careful not to say too much,* she reminded herself.

"Of course. So there are no plans to visit?" she asked.

Josephine did not want the rumormongers of Paris to know the depth of Napoleon's devotion to her or that he had rented a small chateau near hers. "Letters suffice, thank you," she said. Her hand rested atop a plain wooden box on the table beside her. "It is all here— everything I could remember about my life, Madame."

"I am honored, Madame, and of course, I will honor your request," she said, leaning forward. "Your secrets shall be safe with me."

"Until I am gone," Josephine said.

"One hopes that will not occur for many years, my dear, but nothing will be published until you are gone. You have my solemn oath on that."

Josephine sighed and took a sip of her tea. "There is one incident I believe you will find most interesting as it falls within your particular realm of expertise—an encounter with a fortuneteller on Martinique when I was a young girl. I never mentioned it to anyone before now. She told my cousin and me that we would both be queens."

"Queens? Surely, you do not mean to say that you have a cousin who is also a queen."

"Yes, although not a queen in the traditional sense." She smiled tentatively and took another sip of tea before continuing.

"We were both fourteen years old when we visited an old *obeah* woman, a fortune-teller you would call her. She was legendary among the Creoles because her predictions always came true, and we were desperate to know if we would marry."

"Was she a gypsy?"

"No. *Obeah* is an African word. She practiced *Vodoun* magic, and we called her a witch. She was actually the half-African and half-Irish daughter of a slave who bewitched an Irish plantation owner. That was what everyone said, anyway." Josephine shivered and pulled her cloak closer around her shoulders. "Her name was Euphemia David. They called her the Irish Pythoness."

Mlle. Le Normand's eyes widened. "Was it common practice for people to consult with her?"

"Yes, for the Creoles. It was forbidden to me, as a Catholic. But you know, so many Catholic men married Creole women—like my father—and those Creole roots went deep. Our visit was quite the clandestine outing, arranged with the help of a young slave girl."

Josephine took a sheaf of old, yellowed papers from the box. "The day after we saw her, I wrote down everything she had said." She carefully opened the aged pages and glanced at them. "I never discussed that night again with my cousin Aimée, because the predictions for her were so horrid. I hoped she would forget and prayed they would not come to pass."

Mlle. Le Normand sat forward onto the edge of the settee, resting the fan in her lap. "But did they come to pass?"

Josephine answered softly, "Yes."

Mlle. Le Normand reached forward to pat Josephine's hand. "Well, let us discuss your good fortune then, hmmm? What were her predictions for young Josephine?"

Josephine coughed and took a sip of tea. "Firstly, my name was not Josephine. My given name was Marie-Josèphe Rose Tascher de La Pagerie, but everyone called me Rose. Bonaparte changed my name to Josephine before we married."

Mlle. Le Normand's eyebrows raised. "I did not know that."

"You also did not know that he changed the spelling of his own name from the Corsican Buonoparte to the more French sounding Bonaparte."

"*Mon dieu*. You are a font of information today, my dear."

Josephine smiled. "There is much you do not know, old friend, and that I intend to remedy."

"Please tell more of the old fortuneteller."

"It was late one summer night, and Aimée and I secretly left my house like thieves in our nightdresses. We crept through the dark jungle to the *obeah's* shack, and we were both so frightened. The old woman bade us sit on the floor before her, and as we did we saw the tiny white bones she cast onto the floor while she smoked her pipe."

"Her pipe?"

Josephine laughed. "Oh yes, she smoked a long clay pipe, and then she looked at us and told us not to be afraid and that she was honored by our visit. Her eyes were perhaps the strangest thing about her, the palest green. She threw the bones for me and immediately said that I would marry."

Mlle. Le Normand raised her hand dismissively and

made a *"phtt"* sound with her mouth. "Any fool could have told you that," she said.

"Oh no, she was quite specific, Madame. She went on to say that I would marry a man originally destined to be the husband of another in my family, a girl who was doing to die."

"And you had sisters?"

"Yes, I was elated and horrified at the same time. I have never ceased to regret that my sister Catherine's death brought my first husband to me. Although, having known his true disposition, her death may have been a kinder fate than mine."

Mlle. Le Normand *tsk*-ed, and shook her head. "Yes, poor man. A victim of the revolution."

"You misunderstand, Madame. He was a cad and a wastrel—unfit to be either husband or father. I was in the process of divorcing him when he was imprisoned and beheaded. But that is another story about which I have also written." She patted the wooden box. "Euphemia David said nothing of his character whatsoever. She said that a legal proceeding would separate us and that he would perish tragically, leaving me a widow with two children."

"Ah, yes, your children, Eugène and Hortense."

Josephine riffled through her notes. "She spoke of my second marriage, and what she said of Bonaparte was truly intriguing. She said when we met he would be without fortune. Can you imagine a poor Bonaparte?" Both women laughed. "And yet, he was indeed poor when I married him. Lastly, she said that he would rule the world."

"She seems quite the gifted seer, Madame."

"Yes, she said many things, all sounding too fantastic to ever come to pass and yet, they all came true. She said that upon my departure from Martinique a flame of light would appear in the sky. She called it a 'harbinger of my destiny.'"

"But surely, that did not take place."

"Oh yes, it was the most frightening and extraordinary thing. The day I set sail from Martinique, blue flames engulfed the mast of the ship! We thought it would set the ship afire, but it did not. The sailors called it Saint Elmo's Fire."

"I have heard of this phenomenon, but never witnessed it. My goodness. More tea, Madame?"

As Mlle. Le Normand refilled their cups, Josephine silently read her notes. Her face looked pained, and she spoke almost too quietly to be heard. "She concluded by telling me that I would die alone and miserable."

"Oh my dear, regardless of our accomplishments, we all die alone, do we not? Alone does not necessarily indicate that one is miserable." She *tsk*-ed again and patted Josephine's hand. "What of your cousin's fate? Why did her prediction upset you so?"

"I tried to make light of it for poor Aimée's sake, told her it was just superstitious drivel. Now, I can hardly believe that it actually happened. Had I not made these notes the next day, I might not have remembered at all." She coughed for a few moments, then regained her breath and took a sip of tea. "Forgive me. She was to be abducted by pirates."

Mlle. Le Normand was stunned into silence.

"When the news of her abduction reached us, everyone assumed she was dead. She had been in a convent for several years, intending to take her vows and become a nun. How would an innocent girl like that ever survive capture by ruthless pirates? I secretly prayed she would not. Only I knew of the prediction, that Aimée would face a fate worse than death." Her hands shook as she consulted her notes. "You see, she was sold into the Ottoman Sultan's harem, just as the *obeah* woman said."

Mlle. Le Normand's hand pressed against her chest. "Oh, pray no! This came to pass?"

Josephine carefully refolded the papers. "I am afraid so."

"Is the girl still alive?" she whispered.

"Yes, very much so. I received a letter from her only a few weeks ago. We have been corresponding for many years, since she was first able to send word from Istanbul."

"Imprisoned in a seraglio? Like Monsieur Mozart's opera?" Mlle. Le Normand whispered.

Josephine leaned forward and gently touched Mlle. Le Normand's forearm. "She does not consider it a prison, Madame, and her son is now the Sultan of the Ottoman Empire."

The older woman's mouth dropped open. "A Frenchwoman? How extraordinary."

Josephine leaned back and smiled. "Extraordinary does not begin to describe it, Madame. You would not believe the life my cousin Aimée has lived. That is a story I wish I knew more of. You may write what there is of it with mine if you like."

August 1, 1812

> *My dearest Rose,*
>
> *At long last I am able to write with good news. After six terrible years of strife, our war with Russia is finally over. I sincerely hope our victory does not prove to be France's loss, nor produce deleterious effects upon you or the people of France. Why can empires not learn to live in peace? Perhaps we have lived with war for too long, and peace feels unfamiliar. Despite the new stability, the menace of revolution still surrounds us, though most people here seem greatly satisfied with Mahmud and the progress he has brought.*
>
> *As you may remember, my responsibilities reach far beyond the palace walls and I have been immersed in plans for more public buildings than you can imagine: schools, hospitals, baths and libraries. In a few years, I think all of Istanbul will be new and modern. Our first school for girls already has more than two hundred students. I am thrilled that French language and history have been added to many curriculums. I have no doubt Mahmud will one day exceed even the accomplishments of his cousin Selim.*
>
> *How are your children and grandchildren? Is Hortense still in France? What news of Eugène? Are you enjoying your country home or do you miss the excitement of Paris?*
>
> *I pray that peace remains a constant for us all.*
> *Your loving cousin,*
> *Aimée*

Nakshidil could not have known that eleven days later, Russia would sign a second peace treaty with another long-time enemy, Great Britain. In Czar Alexander's opinion, neither the Ottoman nor British Empires posed as dangerous a threat as Napoleon.

Less than one month later, Napoleon's army marched into Moscow, with devastating results. Most dwellings were destroyed, one third of the inhabitants were killed and the resulting fires burned for six days. It would have been a victory for Napoleon if not for an astounding discovery — an official copy of the Treaty of Bucharest signed one month earlier by Russia and Great Britain. The revelation meant that British troops were already on the march towards Russia, and there would be no easy occupation or retreat for the French army. Napoleon's only hope would be to sue for peace. Two weeks of talks ensued and ultimately proved to be fruitless. No agreements were reached, leaving retreat as the only option.

Towards the end of October, Napoleon's army began retreating from Moscow. It was not yet winter, which initially seemed a good omen.

Chapter 23

"France seems to have turned cold towards its Emperor," Sultan Mahmud said as he entered his mother's sitting room and handed her a newspaper. It was the latest edition of the *Paris Moniteur*. "This was written by Napoleon's first consul," he added. Nakshidil read:

Bonaparte's character presents many unaccountable incongruities. Although the most positive man that perhaps ever existed, yet there never was one who more readily yielded to the charm of illusion. In many circumstances the wish and the reality were to him one and the same thing. He never indulged in greater illusions than at the beginning of the campaign of Moscow. Even before the approach of the disasters, which accompanied the most fatal retreat recorded in history, all sensible persons concurred that the Emperor ought to have passed the winter of 1812-13 in Poland, and have resumed his vast enterprises in the spring. But his natural impatience impelled him forward, under the influence of an invisible demon stronger than even his own strong will. This demon was ambition.

He who knew so well the value of time, never sufficiently understood its power, nor how much may be gained by delay. Caesar did not conquer Gaul in one campaign. Another illusion by which Napoleon was misled during the campaign of Moscow was the belief that the Emperor Alexander would propose peace when he saw him at the head of his army on the Russian territory. Bonaparte's prolonged stay at Moscow can be accounted for in no other way than by supposing he expected the Russian cabinet would change its opinion and consent to treat for peace. However, after his long and useless stay in Moscow, Napoleon left that city with the design of taking up his winter quarters in Poland; but Fate now frowned upon Napoleon. In that dreadful retreat the elements seemed leagued with the Russians to destroy the most formidable army ever commanded by one chief. To find a catastrophe in history comparable to that of the Beresina we must go back to the destruction of the legions of Varus in AD 9.

Nakshidil put the paper down and asked "What exactly is Beresina?"

"It is a river that separates Poland from Russia. My advisors say it should have been frozen in late November, when they were meant to cross, but it was not. The unexpected delay cost him an untold number of men and all his cannon."

"How terrible," she said. "It seems that Napoleon escaped with his life only to have his own people turn against him. How terribly French."

"What do you mean?" he asked.

"My personal experience as a girl in Paris was not a pleasant one. Although, it was part of the reason I am here, for which I am grateful."

"Will you tell me more of this, Mother? I know so little about your past."

"Of course I will someday. At the moment, I am more concerned with the current events in France."

~ ~ ~

On February 26, 1813 Russian troops began marching through Austria towards Prussia. Despite the Austrians' agreement to support Napoleon, no Austrian troops gave any challenge to the Russians. The first Cossacks were seen in the village of Bergdorf, north of Hamburg, and each town capitulated gladly to them from fear. By the time Napoleon had rebuilt his army back up to 180,000 men, Russians occupied all the towns through which the French army had to pass.

The bitterness and determination against Napoleon's seemingly unquenchable thirst for power and dominance caused unification throughout Europe. Countries that had been enemies for hundreds of years banded together to fight their common enemy. The sequence of defeats throughout 1813 eventually brought an end to Napoleon's era of domination.

During the first three months of 1814, Napoleon's armies were defeated on every front. On the fourteenth of March, the final blow was struck, when Austria, Russia, Prussia and Great Britain signed the Treaty of Chaumont that would bind them together in peace for twenty years—against Napoleon.

May 19, 1814

My dearest, dear Aimée,
Wonderful news at last! Once again it seems extraordinary happiness has come from terrible loss. As you may already know, Napoleon has suffered a final defeat at the hands

of our own countrymen. The alliance of our enemies proved deadly, and he was forced to abdicate and go into exile on the island of Elba. He departed last month, but without his wife and son, who were meant to join him forthwith. She now refuses to accompany him in exile and has fled France to rejoin her family (and some say her lover) in Austria. What wife deserts her husband at such a time unless she is the most selfish and hateful of women? (Which he says she is). To take the child from him is particularly cruel, as the boy is his only true-born son and heir.

This would all be terrible news indeed if not for the fact that Napoleon has asked me to join him! Just writing those words fills me with joy. Of course I have agreed and feel happier and more excited than I have since leaving Martinique. Leaving France will not be difficult, as I have already endured the past four years in exile. Now, both of our exiles shall end with our reunion. However much time may be left to us shall be spent in joyous union together. And, dear cousin, we will live on a delightfully secluded island, just as we grew up, without the bonds of politics, government or society. As you said in your letter, "We are no longer young," and must be grateful for the gifts we have. Napoleon has always been one of my most precious gifts, and I believe him when he says the same of me.

I sail to join him two weeks hence and shall post a letter to you when I arrive, with instructions for posting to me. There is much to do.

Wish me well, dearest cousin, pray to the God that hears you, and know that I shall be happy again at last!

Ever your loving cousin,

Rose

Aimée was thrilled for Rose. This would truly be life's best gift to her. She wished she could write back immediately to tell her how excited she was, and realized she must tell Mahmud.

"Come take a walk in the garden with me," she said. "There are some things I want to tell you."

"Not another dire prediction from a fortuneteller, I hope."

"Not dire and not a prediction. Just a bit of family history—my family in France."

They walked into the Sultan's private gardens, past a tranquil pond, and sat on a marble bench beneath a weeping willow tree.

"I've had a letter from my cousin, Rose, The Empress Josephine," she began.

"I always find it interesting that you call her Rose," he said.

"Did you know that she still calls me Aimée?"

He gave her a quizzical look. "I did not."

The Valide Sultana smiled. "Before I came to this place, my name was Marie-Marthé Aimée Dubucq de Rivery."

"Why have you never told me this?" he asked.

"I had no reason before now. It occurs to me that one day you may wish to travel to France, and if you should, you would have the opportunity to meet members of my family—your cousins. Rose and I have meant so much to each other all our lives. Perhaps one day you will meet one of *your* cousins through our bloodline, and he may become part of your life as Rose is a part of mine."

"Cousins," he said thoughtfully. "I never realized that I have no family except you."

"Not here, but you do in France. You've always shown such an affinity for France and all things French. Why not visit the country itself and meet your French relatives?"

"Why not indeed?" he replied. "What an extraordinary idea." She had given him something to ponder. *Are all Sultans without family except for children?*

"I'll write down as much of my family history as I can recall. It reaches far beyond France. Rose's daughter, Hortense de Beauharnais, married Emperor Napoleon's brother Joseph. Until recently, they were King and Queen of Holland. Her son, Eugène, is a prince of Venice and married a princess of Bavaria. They have several children...all your cousins. One never knows how or when such connections may be useful to a ruler like yourself, with eyes on the West."

"As always, Mother, you are correct, and I look forward to learning about these relatives and, perhaps one day, meeting them. An extraordinary idea," he repeated.

"You have French blood in your veins as well as Ottoman, and both serve you well. Why not walk in both worlds?"

"Why not, indeed," he replied.

"I am sorry that your cousin Selim is not here with us," she said.

"Yes, I miss him too, and he would be so excited by the progress we are making."

"He was easily excited by so many things," she said wistfully.

Mahmud watched her face intently. "Did you love him?" he asked.

"Yes, Mahmud. I loved him very much."

~ ~ ~

With plans to embark for the island of Elba on June first, Josephine went happily about the tremendous task of packing her home and possessions, deciding what to take, what to sell and what to leave in the house. There were meetings with her solicitors and financial advisors, and all manner of letters of instructions for maintaining the house during her absence. Hortense brought the children to Malmaison for the final weeks, and planned to live there whenever she was not in Paris. Everyone was sworn to secrecy regarding the move, as the former Empress wished to avert direct confrontation with those who might oppose her decision. She also did not wish the news to reach the new Empress Marie-Louise until after she was gone. Who knew what spiteful act that woman might set in motion? That was another reason for haste. Josephine was well aware of how fast gossip spread. The Parisian gossipmongers would eventually feast upon the tasty morsel, but hopefully not until she was gone. For this reason, she avoided any contact with Mlle. Le Normand and went about her organizing and packing in high spirits, despite the onset of an annoying cough.

~ ~ ~

By mid-July, it was too hot to stroll in her private gardens so instead, Nakshidil Sultana bathed in an outdoor cool-water pool. She was stretched out on the soft grass at the pool's edge, partially covered with a light cloth, when Perestu arrived excitedly waving a letter. "From France," she said happily. "It came by special messenger, and I thought you would want to see it right away."

"Oh, good. I've been waiting to hear from her." She sat up and excitedly tore the letter open. She read the first line and her face crumbled into tears. Crushing the letter to her breast she sobbed, "No, no. Rose, not Rose."

Perestu knelt to wrap her arms around her sobbing friend and gently took the letter from her hands. She read, *It is with great sadness that I write to inform you of the death of my mother, your cousin, the Empress Josephine.*

"Rose," Perestu whispered. She continued reading silently. *Amidst preparations to leave France and join her beloved Napoleon in exile, she contracted pneumonia, and passed from this world in three days' time, on twenty nine May.* She scanned the rest of the letter to the end and saw that it was signed by Rose's daughter, Hortense. "Oh, Namay, I am so sorry."

"Why Rose? Why now? She was so excited to reunite with Napoleon—was so happy," she sobbed. "Why could she not have happiness?"

"I do not know. I think maybe only God knows," Perestu said.

"What God?" Nakshidil said angrily. "Why would any God do this? What God chooses to make our lives a misery?"

"But Namay, your life is wonderful," Perestu replied. "God has given you so many gifts."

"And taken so many from me as well," she said bitterly.

The Valide dried her tears with the edge of the blanket. "Taken more than you know, dear friend." She sighed heavily and looked directly into the younger woman's eyes. "You are the only friend left to me now, little bird. You and Mahmud are all I have left. Everyone I have ever loved has been taken from me. Everyone." She began to weep again as snippets of memories played in her mind's eye—Rose, Mihrisah and Selim. *All gone.* She took in a slow deep breath to quiet her tears then released it with a sigh. "Save for the two of you, I am alone."

"My dearest Namay, was it not you who taught me that we are all truly alone?" Perestu asked. "You said we are born alone and die alone, with only God beside us."

Nakshidil thought about it a moment. "I suppose we are, my dear." She patted the younger woman's hands and repeated. "I suppose we are."

The realization that Rose was truly gone began to seep deeper into Aimée's consciousness as another wave of sorrow brought more tears. Perestu gently stroked her sobbing friend's shoulders and back.

When the grip of sadness subsided the older woman looked into the younger's deep brown eyes and asked, "When did you become so wise, little bird?"

"When I lost the first person I ever loved," she answered.

Nakshidil nodded. "Of course." The thought of Selim brought a bittersweet smile to her lips. "I loved him too, you know."

"Yes, I suspected as much and was glad of it. Selim needed all of our love."

"He *deserved* our love, little bird. And now, Rose is gone too. Poor Rose. What a cruel turn of fate."

"Yes," Perestu said, "*Kismet* is not always kind."

"Ah, *kismet*. We expect that it always brings us together but it also tears us apart." The Valide took a deep breath and then smiled at her young friend. "I am grateful it brought you to me; one day it will take me too."

"Not for a long time, I hope. Your life is so very happy now."

A puzzled look came over the Sultana's face. "What did the old woman say?" she mused.

"What old woman?" Perestu asked.

"The old *obeah* woman, Euphemia David."

Perestu looked at her quizzically. "What do you mean?" she asked. "I do not know these words."

Aimée was lost in reverie, remembering the tiny shack in the jungle, and two young girls sitting on the floor. She could hear the old woman's gravelly voice saying, *when you t'ink yourself da most happy, a wasting sickness will take you away.* "Do you think me to be truly very happy?" she asked aloud.

"I do Naksh. Your son sits on the throne, and you have everything your heart desires. The people love you both because you have given them so much to be grateful for. Why would you not be happy?"

The Sultana listened to her friend's words intently. "Well then," she said, feeling distinctly calmer than she had a moment before. "I believe you are correct. And if I am indeed 'the most happy,' I had best enjoy it. Who can know how long it will last? If I've learned any lesson well in this life it is that nothing lasts forever. All we ever truly possess is each moment."

Epilogue

In the winter of 1817, following nine years of her son's peaceful reign, Nakshidil Sultana, the former Marie-Marthé Aimée Dubucq de Rivery, contracted pneumonia. At her request, her son led a blindfolded Catholic priest into her private apartments within the seraglio to administer last rites. She passed peacefully in her sleep that night, at fifty-four years old. As Valide Sultana, Nakshidil built more than fifty public buildings in Istanbul, including the French Library, public schools, public baths, fountains, hospitals, mosques and food kitchens for the poor. Aimée Dubucq de Rivery would never become famous, but Ottoman history would forever remember Nakshidil, The French Sultana, the woman who changed an empire. Her direct descendants ruled the Ottoman Empire in a continuous line from her son, Mahmud, through the last Ottoman Sultan, Abdul-Majid Kahn II, who was deposed on March 3, 1924, when the sultancy was dissolved. Descendants of the Imperial House of Osman continue to this day, and carry the title of Prince.

~ ~ ~

The Empress Josephine de Beauharnais Bonaparte, née Marie-Joseph Rose Tascher de la Pagerie, was buried in the churchyard of St. Pierre—St. Paul church in Rueil-Malmaison. In 1852 her grandson, Hortense's third son, was crowned Emperor Napoleon III. He ruled France successfully for two decades, then led it to defeat in the Franco-German War and died two years later.

Eugène de Beauharnais retired to his father-in-law Maximilian's estates in Bavaria following Napoleon's exile, and gave up politics. His six children married into the royal families of Sweden, Germany, Russia, Brazil and Portugal.

Josephine's daughter, Hortense de Beauharnais Bonaparte, retired to her estate in Arenenberg, Switzerland, where she died in 1837. She was survived by only two of her four sons.

~ ~ ~

Following Napoleon's abdication and banishment, the French (Bourbon) monarchy was restored in 1814 with King Louis XVIII.

In March of 1815, Napoleon escaped from Elba and returned to Paris, where he reclaimed his title in a period known as The Hundred Days. Three months later he was defeated at the Battle of Waterloo, which brought an end to the French domination of Europe. He abdicated for a second time and was this time exiled to the remote island of Saint Helena, in the southern Atlantic Ocean, where he lived until his death on May 5, 1821. The cause of death originally believed to be either stomach cancer or arsenic poisoning, still remains a mystery. Although modern DNA testing revealed trace amounts of arsenic

268 | Zia Wesley

in hair samples, no one was able to definitely identify the samples as being from Napoleon. Also, the amounts were far too small to indicate arsenic as a cause of death. Napoleon's only legitimate son, called Napoleon II, never actually acceded to the throne and died in 1832 at the age of twenty-one.

~ ~ ~

In 1820, Marie Le Normand's biography of Josephine, *Historical and Secret Memoirs of the Empress Josephine, Marie Rose Tascher De La Pagerie, First Wife of Napoleon Bonaparte*, was published in France. In 1847, John E. Potter of Philadelphia published an English edition.

~ ~ ~

The mysterious piece of inscribed black basalt discovered in Egypt and brought back to France by Napoleon's troops, was translated by the French linguist Jean Francois Champollion in 1822 and proved to be the key to unlocking Egyptian hieroglyphics. It is known as The Rosetta stone.

~ ~ ~

"The Auspicious Event of 1826" was the bloody and very final end of the Janissaries, engineered by Nakshidil's son, Mahmud II.

~ ~ ~

In 1867, Aimée's grandson, Sultan Abdul Aziz Khan,

became the first Ottoman Sultan to visit France. The following excerpt is from the *Journal de France* dated July 10, 1867:

Sultan Abdul Aziz arrived in Paris this week for a state visit. As the first Ottoman Emperor to visit France, he was given a warm welcome by the government, which provided him with a huge suite at the Elysée Palace and a staff to assist his own vast retinue of servants. Among the Sultan's wishes were hardboiled eggs at breakfast, Napoleon pastries at lunch, chocolates in the evening and private performances in his suite by the girls from the Folies Bergère. When asked why he had invited Sultan Abdul Aziz to Paris, Emperor Louis Napoleon replied he was most curious to meet Sultan Abdul Aziz because "we are related through our grandmothers."

~ ~ ~

Napoleon's chief engineer, Jacques La Pere had been wrong about the height difference between the Red Sea and the Mediterranean and on April 25, 1859 work on the modern Suez Canal began. It took ten years and one hundred million dollars to complete and opened on November 17, 1869. The original canal dated back to the thirteenth century BC.

~ ~ ~

The alliance between Muhammad Ibn Abd al-Wahhab and Muhammad Ibn Saud, head of the Al Saud tribal family, which was forged in 1804, still exists to this day. In 1902, a direct descendent of Muhammad Ibn Saud, twenty-year-old Abd al-Aziz Ibn Saud, rode out of the desert with a small band of brothers and cousins and joined forces with an army of nomadic Bedouins who were Wahhabi puritans known as the Ikhwan. Together, they reclaimed the ancient capital of Riyadh. In 1924 and 1925 they took back the holy cities of Mecca and Medina from the Turks. In 1932, Abd al-Aziz Ibn Saud declared himself king, giving his name to the lands he had captured: Saudi Arabia. To ensure the solidarity of his kingdom, he married one daughter from each of twenty influential Arab tribes. More than twenty sons issued from these unions and countless numbers of grandsons would follow. To this day, every Saudi King has been a son of Abd al-Aziz Ibn Saud.

In 1933, Saudi Arabia and the United States of America signed an agreement for oil exploration, and later created Aramco, the Arabian American Oil Company, whose shareholders include America's four largest oil corporations.

Historical Facts

Sultan Selim III entered history as "The Great Modernizer."

Nakshidil's son, Sultan Mahmud II reigned for thirty-one years, from 1808 to 1839, and instituted radical Western changes into Turkish society. He outlawed turbans and kaftans, replacing them with frock coats and the fez, introduced dining on chairs, the use of eating utensils, Western foods and alcoholic beverages such as champagne and brandy. He also reformed outdated protocols both social and governmental, replacing them with Western-style manners and government. He entered history as Mahmud the Reformer and sired 43 children, of which two became Sultans: the eldest, Sultan Abdul Majid Khan I, followed by Abdul Aziz Kahn I.

Eugene de Beauharnais' children:

Princess Joséphine Maximiliane Eugénie Napoléone de Beauharnais (1807–1876) became the Queen Consort to King Oscar I of Sweden, himself the son of Napoleon's old love, Désirée Clary.

Princess Eugénie Hortense Auguste de Beauharnais (1808–1847) married Friedrich, Prince of Hohenzollern-Hechingen.

Prince Auguste Charles Eugène Napoléon de Beau-harnais (1810–1835), 2nd Duke of Leuchtenberg, married Queen Maria II of Portugal.

Princess Amélie Auguste Eugénie Napoléone de Beauharnais (1812–1873) was the second wife of Peter I of Brazil, and became Empress.

Princess Theodelinde Louise Eugénie Auguste Na-poléone de Beauharnais (1814–1857) married Wilhelm, 1st Duke of Urach.

Prince Maximilian Josèphe Eugène Auguste Napo-léon de Beauharnais (1817–1852) married Grand Duch-ess Maria Nikolaievna of Russia, eldest daughter of Tsar Nicholas I, and received the title of "Prince Roma-novsky."

Hortense de Beauharnais Bonaparte's children:

Charles Louis Napoléon Bonaparte (1808–1873) be-came Emperor Napoleon III from 1852 to 1870.

Charles Auguste Louis Joseph Demorny (1811–1865), her illegitimate son by Auguste Charles Joseph, Comte de Flahaut de La Billarderie (1785–1870), was born secretly in Switzerland. He became a political and social leader during the Second Empire, after playing an important role in the coup d'etat of 1851, that led to his half-brother's nomination as Emperor Napoleon III.

Napoleon's second wife, The Empress Marie-Louise, married twice after his death; both times morganatical-ly—meaning that neither spouse nor offspring could in-herit royal titles or monies. Her second husband was

Count Adam Albert von Neipperg, an "equerry" she met in 1814, who fathered her two children. The 1814 Treaty of Fontainebleau handed over the Duchies of Parma, Piacenza and Guastalla to Marie-Louise, which she ruled until her death.

Glossary

Ada: a depilatory paste made from beet sugar or honey and lemon.

Al-Djazir: The old translation of the city name for Algiers.

Ambergris: a solid waxy substance produced by whales that was used in perfumes and fragrant incense.

Arak: an anise flavored liquor.

Barbarosa: the nickname given to Hayreddin Pasha by Europeans. It means "red beard" in Italian and Spanish. He was the Admiral of the fleet under Suleiman the Magnificent in 1478-1546 and entered history a notorious pirate.

Baskadine: mother of the first-born heir to the sultan's throne.

Baskatibe: the first secretary who was responsible for discipline and conduct in the harem.

Bakshish: bribes or payoffs sometimes disguised as "tribute".

Bey or **Beg**: a provincial governor.

Bursa: healing water.

Caftan or **Kaftan**: the long robe with wide sleeves worn by men and women.

Camasr Usta: ran the laundry and cared for imperial robes. The basins and clotheslines used for the sultan's robes were always silver.

Cariye: the name for novices and slaves.

Cariye darisi: school for odalisks.

Chief taster: tasted the sultan's food for poison. She wore red trousers and a long gown with a yellow handkerchief.

Corps of Gardeners/gardeners: elite assassins employed to eliminate the sultan's enemies at his command.

Dey: an honorary title given to a ruler of an entire territory or province.

The Divan: The Ottoman government.

Ferace: the traditional covering worn by Moslem women throughout the Ottoman Empire. Made of silk in summer and heavier cloth in winter, the lower classes always wore black while upper classes wore a wide variety of bright colors.

Grand Vizier: the defacto head of state in the seventeenth century. The Sultan's most primary official who held power of attorney and presided over the government in the sultan's absence. There were eleven viziers under the Grand Vizier.

The Hall of the Divan: The opulent reception hall where the sultan received his guests.

Hamam: communal Turkish baths.

Ibriktar Usta: the superintendant of the baths (hamam).

Janissaries: Christian boys taken from their families at five or six years of age who were converted to Islam and trained as "soldiers of Allah". They served as members of the Ottoman army, navy, police force and palace guards.

Jezve: traditional coffee pot.

Kafes or **Cage**: A three story windowless building built in 1603 that was guarded by deaf mutes and used to protect/incarcerate heirs to the throne.

Kalfa: older serving women.

Kizlar Agasi: Referred to by Turkish people as "the Pasha with three tails" he was a black eunuch who ruled the harem with the sultana or sultan valide. His responsibilities included filling vacancies in the harem, the education of heirs, the sentencing and execution of women who committed crimes, overseeing the investments of the favorites, the inspection of charitable institutions and was a confidential messenger of the sultan. He accumulated immense wealth and owned slaves, horses and eunuchs.

Kutuchu Usta: herbalists who served as pharmacists to the harem women. Assisted their mistresses at eh baths, wardrobes, and hair. Used herbs and unguents, pediatric medical practices unknown in Europe such as vaccinations, and assisted in pregnancies and childbirth. Often engaged in poisonings.

Malmaison: The Empress Josephine's estate in the city of Rueil seven miles outside of Paris.

Maymay: Rose's pet name for Aimée.

Nargileh: water pipes for smoking a mixture of herbs and tobacco.

Odalisque or **odalisk**: the European term for the sultan's women.

Pattens: high wooden shoes that harem women wore in the baths to protect their feet from the residue of depilatories.

Regicide: the practice of killing off heirs to the throne.

Saray Usta: the mistress of ceremonies who oversaw all births, weddings, circumcisions official and religious celebrations. Presided over every ceremony and instructed everyone in behavior they should adopt in the presence of the sultan and imperial family.

Serbet: a frozen sherbet drink made with snow from Mt. Olympus and served in the Sultan's harem. Flavored with flower and fruit essences, they were never available anywhere else due to the great expense of transporting the ice.

Sublime Porte: The Ottoman government.

Sultan Valide: the woman who governed the harem with her close circle of ministers, usually the mother of the heir.

Topkapi Palace: The sultan's palace in Istanbul.

Tressed Halbrediers: young boys whose job it was to bring wood to the harem. They wore two locks of false hair like long curtains, from helmets that shielded their eyes from seeing peripherally so they could not see the harem women.

Ulema: A group of scholarly Islamic priests who played an important part in the Ottoman government. The word Ulema is also used as a title for the most senior of these priests.

Yasmak: the face mask worn by Moslem women usually of fine muslin or silk in two pieces; one covered the mouth and nose, the other wrapped around the head to cover everything except their eyes.

Yeyette: the pet name Rose's family called her.

Vodoun: the French spelling for Voodoo.

About the Author

Zia Wesley is the author of *The Stolen Girl*, the first book in the Veil and the Crown series. She is also the best-selling author of six non-fiction books on natural beauty and longevity writing as Zia Wesley Hosford. Her latest books in this genre include: *Zia's M.A.P. (Master Anti-aging Plan) to Basic Skin Care, Zia's M.A.P. to Growing Young* and *Zia's M.A.P. to Men's Skin Care*. They are currently available online through all of your favorite e book sites.

You can follow Zia on her website and social media for updates and more information about the Veil and the Crown Series.

For a bibliography of the research Zia used in writing the Veil and the Crown series, please go to her website **www.ziawesleynovelist.com/**.

Facebook
www.facebook.com/zia.wesley.1

Twitter
twitter.com/ziawesleynovels

Pinterest
www.pinterest.com/ziawesleynovels/

And email Zia to sign up for all her social media outlets
zia@ziawesleynovelist.com

Made in the USA
San Bernardino, CA
27 February 2017